THE RULE OF 3

The Rule of 3

ARIELLA TALIX

Ringmaster Publishing

Contents

Chapter One

Tanner Lassiter and Zoë Deliban had history.

Tanner was a year ahead of his sister Madison and her best friend Zoë in school, and they all grew up together in a tiny town in southeastern Kentucky named Honeybee Hollow. Zoë had harbored a crush on Tanner from about the age of six when he told her she looked cute with no front teeth. After that, the boy could do no wrong in her eyes.

When she was thirteen, it was Tanner who saw to it that she had her first kiss.

When she was fifteen, he demonstrated how to French kiss. She thanked him by letting him feel up her pretty new breasts.

When she was sixteen, and Tanner had just turned eighteen, they decided to lose their virginity together. It was actually a fairly exciting experience for both of them, so they decided to keep practicing. And they got pretty good at it.

Tanner's mother worked all day at the town library, and his father was a country vet who was busy long, long hours, so that left the house free for teenage shenanigans.

When Zoë was seventeen, Tanner left for Princeton, and she was left to finish high school at Honeybee Hollow High. Tanner announced to Zoë before he left, "We need to make a clean break of it so we can both enjoy college to its fullest."

Zoë assumed that meant Tanner wanted to screw around with lots of pretty Princeton girls, and the thought made her ill. She smiled and kept her tears at bay, though, saying, "I guess you know best, Tanner." Inside, she felt her heart crumble to bits.

She was lonely and heartbroken, and she kept it to herself. Madison was busy with cheerleading and studying when she wasn't with her boyfriend Crunch—the high school football star—so the girls didn't see as much of each other as they had when they were younger.

She skipped her senior prom because, even though three boys had asked her to go, she couldn't stand the idea of some other guy trying to kiss her or feel her up.

Crunch and Madison were Prom King and Queen.

Zoë spent prom night eating ice cream and studying—pretending it was just any night—nothing special. She wanted so badly to call Tanner and see how and what he was doing up at Princeton, but she'd only seen him briefly over the Christmas holiday when he tried to ignore her presence—wounding her to the core. He hadn't come home for spring break.

She needed to get over the stupid feelings she still had for the guy. He wasn't coming back.

****

But he did come back, and that was even worse. After graduating from Princeton, Tanner returned looking like a better version of himself. Taller, now six-foot-one, more chiseled, and way more confident. His hair had grown darker, but he and his beautiful sister shared the same startling blue eyes flecked with green and gold. They both had dazzling smiles and both were intelligent and driven. Madison had plans to start up a business, and Tanner became the youngest-ever mayor of Honeybee Hollow. His personality was infectious, and his confidence made everyone around him feel secure.

Honeybee Hollow was a stepping stone for Tanner's loftier political goals. He just had to wait until he was old enough.

Chapter Two

Tanner loved his years at Princeton. They were exciting and liberating in a way that surprised him. He enjoyed the lively conversations he had with fellow students in a way he'd never been able to achieve in high school.

There were lots and lots of pretty girls to date, and the first few weeks of his freshman year, he'd tried to sample as many as possible. But each time he felt like he might want to become intimate with one of them after their date was winding down, he found himself longing sadly for Zoë's gorgeous brown eyes that used to look at him adoringly. She had shiny, dark hair that tumbled down her back in a fall of silk, and he dreamed about it running through his fingers. Because of her job at the town pool as a lifeguard and swim coach for the younger set, daily exercise and swimming kept her lithe body trim and fit. The kids at the pool adored her.

Tanner chastised himself over and over that she was just a small town, high school girlfriend—not someone he could have a serious adult relationship with. It was ridiculous to consider such a thing. He missed her horribly though. A couple of weeks after school started, he caved in and sent her a text.

Tanner: Hey, I think I might have made a mistake

Zoë: So sorry for you.

Tanner: Well- how are you doing?

Zoë: Fine

Tanner: Can I call you?

Zoë: No

He didn't know what else to say to that and was too young and naïve to realize that when a woman used the word "fine," it meant exactly the opposite. So, he never wrote again or called. On the few occasions they ran into each other when he went home for Christmas and she gave him the cold shoulder, he didn't bother her. He tried to ignore the sadness in her sweet eyes. It was for the best, he told himself.

Sometimes it's tough being a stupid young genius.

***

The first few years he was back in Honeybee Hollow weren't too bad—he was tremendously busy, and Zoë was still away at college getting her teaching credentials. But then she finally returned and took the job of kindergarten teacher at the town elementary school. She was apparently home to stay.

Tanner saw Zoë going about her business in town with the same grace and elegance she'd always had. Children adored her, men of all ages lusted after her, and parents thought she worked magic with their kids. Zoë seemed completely oblivious of her popularity, however. She had always been beautiful, but she had matured into a truly elegant woman.

Tanner still craved her sweetness, but his life was a complicated mess. At Princeton, he had fallen in love, and now he had no idea what to do about it. Tanner was also still in love with Zoë.

Chapter Three

Tanner's favorite class during his first semester was American Politics. He hung on every word the lecturer doled out, but he was distracted by a certain young lady who seemed more fixated on him than political science. She let her interest be known in several ways. Always the southern gentleman, Tanner was unfailingly polite even when he wanted to pay more attention to the lecture than to her.

Monica was short and stacked. She had platinum blonde hair and big brown eyes that would have been doe-like on anyone else, but on her they looked calculating. She was far from Tanner's type. She was too small, too bosomy, and too loud for his taste, but he was becoming so horny he could barely think.

She plunked herself down next to him right before class began on Monday and announced, "I want you to go to a Halloween party with me this Friday night." He looked at her. She sidled closer to him and pressed her boob against his arm. "I'll make you really happy if you go with me."

Tanner got the message, cleared his throat, and answered, "Sure, why not?" and he turned his face away toward the lectern, completely forgetting about Monica's existence until the lecture was over and she slipped him a piece of paper that had her dorm room and phone number on it.

"See you Friday at eight?" she asked and then licked her lips.

Tanner blinked in momentary confusion and then remembered what she wanted. "Eight sounds fine," he answered. "I'll be there."

"Don't forget to wear a costume. I'm going to be a sexy witch," she giggled.

Tanner gave a momentary frown, wondering how a witch could be sexy. He had a vision of the green-faced old crone from *The Wizard of Oz*. Then he wondered what on earth he could do to pull a costume together. "Okay...?" he answered. *Well, something will come to mind, I guess.*

It turned out that Monica's costume looked far more sexy than witchy. Tanner feared she'd come down with a chest cold, her boobs were so exposed. Her black dress was extremely low cut and completely exposed her cleavage through a lace-up front that was open all the way down to her belly button. Her tits looked to Tanner like inflated balloons that were trying to escape their doubtful confines. The dress was roughly the length of a tennis skirt, and her legs were covered in fishnet stocking and knee-high boots. The only thing that provided any authenticity to her claim of being a witch was that she carried a broom.

Tanner was completely unaffected by her outfit, but what he did react to was that she'd covered her platinum hair with a long, black wig. Tanner's eyes dilated, and he felt himself growing hard.

"What on earth are you supposed to be?" Monica asked in a pouty voice. She looked him up and down with an air of incredulity.

Tanner stood in her doorway, dressed in his best suit and a red tie. "It's not obvious?" he asked. Then he waved a cigar in her face. "You were actually my inspiration, *Monica*."

"Uh..." Monica had no clue.

"I'm president!" he laughed.

"Oh... Bill Clinton?" She finally caught on.

"No," he said in a serious tone. "That was a good guess with the cigar, but I just like them. I'm *President Lassiter*."

Squinting at him, Monica stated, "I don't remember a president with that name."

"Not yet," Tanner smirked. "Just give it time. Let's go, beautiful." He was gratified to see Monica grab a coat.

*****

The party was held at one of the eating clubs on The Street at one edge of the campus. It was crammed with bodies. All of the guests had red, plastic cups that they drank from as often as they sloshed their refreshments on the floor and each other. The smell of cheap beer was almost overpowering. Tanner and Monica wandered around for a while, looking at the stupid excuses everyone had for a costume. The girls mostly tried for "sexy" it seemed, as there were nurses, nuns, princesses, etc., that all looked like the costumes had come from some porn catalog. The guys tended to wear football jerseys, cowboy hats and plaid shirts, or a few more adventurous ones wore scrubs and volunteered to give examinations to all of the girls. It was just lame and predictable to Tanner.

The music was so loud everyone had to shout, and no one could decipher what anyone else said most of the time. When Monica asked Tanner where he was from, he answered with a questioning look, "No I don't play drums. Why did you ask that?"

"No, *from*, Tanner! Where did you grow up? You have the cutest accent," she said straight into his ear this time.

Wincing at her loud voice directly in his ear, he said, "Oh, sorry. I misunderstood you. It's terribly loud in here. I'm from Honeybee Hollow, Kentucky." Tanner wasn't about to shout in her ear, so he addressed the room loudly.

"Well, honey yourself," she purred. "You want me to fuck you?" she asked with a wink. "I thought you'd never ask."

"No, not *honey, fuck me*, Honeybee Hollow, Kentucky!"

Monica furrowed her brows, only getting the gist that he'd said no to fucking, but she brightened immediately when someone poured something new into her cup. She took a drink and gasped. She set down her cup and grabbed his tie, pulling him down to her level. "Do you want to get out of here?" she asked, her brown eyes boring into his.

"Yes," Tanner said, relieved. He'd had enough of this party, even though they'd only been there less than an hour. And he wanted to get his suit cleaned as soon as possible.

Going outdoors was a refreshing change from the deafening, stuffy party, and Tanner took in grateful gulps of chilly air as they made their way back to Monica's dorm. His ears rang, however, and he had the beginning of a headache.

"C'mon in, *honey*," she ordered with a grin when they got to her room. "My roommate is out for the whole night." She took his hand and pulled him through the door. As soon as they got inside, Monica flung off her coat and whipped around to face Tanner. She dropped to her knees and unzipped his pants.

"Wh...?" Tanner was so shocked he didn't even know how to react. But his boner did it all for him. As soon as he looked down and felt her hand grasp his dick and pull it free, he was as stiff as a cement block. The sight of that long dark hair leaning towards him and then the feel of her hot mouth around him almost did him in. He moaned loudly and happily and shoved his fingers roughly into Monica's long black hair.

Unfortunately, the hair was coarse and felt like plastic, and when he grasped it, the wig slipped off. He was left holding it in his hand. His next moan was that of complete horror. He saw platinum hair where there ought to have been brunette, and he dropped the wig on the floor with a soft plop. His boner deflated faster than a whoopee cushion under a hippo.

Tanner stepped back immediately.

Monica looked up at him and asked, "What the fuck? I thought you'd be down for some fun, Tanner."

Looking anywhere but at her, he mumbled, "Sorry," zipped his fly, and made for the door.

On his brisk walk back to his own dorm, he mused, *Well, maybe now she'll leave me alone in class. I feel like a Class A jerk, though.*

Chapter Four

After his walk across campus, back in his room, Tanner was a mess. He removed his smelly, beer-stained suit and pulled on a pair of flannel pants. He crawled into his bed and started to think about Zoë. Shutting his eyes, he remembered her sweet innocence the first time she'd blown him. It was like tonight, only with far better results. She'd dropped to her knees and he'd wrapped her long hair in one hand while he balanced himself with the other hand against the top of his desk chair. He remembered the feel of her silky tresses and her soft lips. He'd cried out in bliss and blown his load down her throat before she'd even gotten going.

Tanner's hand crept into his pants and he began to stroke his erection. Feeling constricted, he stopped, pushed away the blankets, undid his drawstring and shoved his pants down for better access. Spitting into his palm, he grabbed himself again, envisioning Zoë's mouth and her perfect tits. With closed eyes and a hand that was sliding up and down ferociously, Tanner was enjoying his fantasy to the hilt when his roommate Eli opened the door. Eli took two steps into the room, quickly shut the door, and gave Tanner a lascivious grin.

"Want some help with that?" he asked with a nod of his head toward Tanner's crotch.

Expecting a frustrating de-bone number two in one night, Tanner was dumbfounded to realize he was even harder than before. He opened and closed his mouth like a fish. The only sound that finally came out was a croak.

Tanner's roommate, Elison Whittaker, was a legacy Princetonian. His father, grandfather, and great grandfather had all attended the university, and there was never a doubt about whether Eli would get in—not that he wasn't qualified. He was from a prominent New York family that had billions and used them to further their agendas by constantly throwing money at politicians and the media. Eli was tall with black hair and stunning hazel eyes. He was so handsome he was nearly beautiful in a male model kind of way. He also loved to walk around the room with barely any clothes on as often as he could.

It had never bothered Tanner, who really liked the guy from the first day they'd arrived on campus. But Eli's question flabbergasted him. His own reaction to Eli shocked Tanner even more.

Eli's personality was so magnetic, men and women were drawn to him like hummingbirds to nectar. Suddenly, Tanner realized that Eli had been flirting with him all along, and he'd just chalked it up to friendliness and a dislike of clothing in a room that tended toward stuffy in the early fall. The historic old dorm was not air-conditioned, so a lack of clothing had seemed somewhat normal. But now that the temperatures were dropping, Eli still hadn't worn a lot.

Tanner remembered cutting short his dates a few times to hang with Eli, and now understood he'd been affected by Eli subconsciously from the very beginning.

With his mouth still hanging open, and his dick still doing its flagpole impression, Tanner watched as Eli sat down carefully next to him on the bed.

Staring straight into Tanner's eyes, Eli asked softly, "Ever done it with a guy?"

Tanner still just stared and shook his head. His dick was so hard by now, it hurt.

"May I?" asked Eli as he covered Tanner's hand with his own. "You might be surprised at how great it is when someone with the same equipment does it for you." With his other hand, he gently pulled Tanner's hand off. "Say yes, Tanner, and I'll rock your world." He stroked up and down Tanner's shaft as Tanner tore his eyes away to watch the big male hand stroking his dick. He couldn't deny it felt wonderful. "You're so beautiful, Tanner. I've been dying to do this for weeks now. Say yes, please."

Tanner closed his eyes, felt the pressure building and building in his balls, and croaked out, "Yes. Do it!" He didn't know what had come over him, but for some reason it felt more than right. And then his eyes flew open again as he felt a hot, wet mouth engulfing him all the way to his sac. "Ohmygod, Eli!"

Eli shoved Tanner's pants down past his knees and then slid his hand up Tanner's thigh. Swirling his tongue around the hard shaft, Eli stroked Tanner's skin gently and slid his hand between Tanner's legs. He reached up, stroking Tanner's balls gently and then slid his long fingers behind Tanner's scrotum, seeking out his asshole. The entire time, Eli's mouth kept up an intense suction, sliding up and down as his free hand firmly grasped the base of Tanner's erection.

Tanner was beside himself. He'd never in a million years have pictured himself with his dick in some dude's mouth, but it felt amazing. He involuntarily jutted his hips up, seeking more pressure. When he did, he felt strong fingers massaging his ass. This new experience was too much. He succumbed to the tremendous pleasure and cried out in a strangled croak, "Coming!"

Eli chuckled and sucked even harder. He increased the pressure of his fingertips and swallowed as Tanner shook and shuddered, groaning with release. He sucked and sucked until Tanner had no more to give, and then he shocked Tanner one more time.

Eli's mouth released Tanner's cock but he kept his fingers in place, still stroking him. Then he kissed the daylights out of Tanner.

Tanner could taste the salty cum on Eli's tongue and discovered... he liked it. The feel of Eli's rough cheeks against his was a totally new sensation that Tanner immediately enjoyed. He also liked it when Eli stood and pulled off all of his clothes, leaving them in a heap, and climbed back onto the bed, pulling Tanner into his arms. Tanner pulled back for a moment, kicked off his pants the rest of the way and pulled the blanket over them, snuggling back into Eli's embrace.

In the middle of the night, Tanner awoke to the weird sensation of a long, muscular, hairy leg sandwiched between his own two legs. At first it startled him, but then he realized he liked it. It felt strange to be in bed with no pajamas on, but the skin-to-skin contact was comforting and pleasant. The next time he woke up, the hairy leg was gone, and the person it was attached to was snoring lightly across the room. Dorm room beds weren't exactly built for two men their size. Tanner grumbled, pulled on his pajama bottoms, headed for the bathroom to take a leak, and looked at himself in the mirror. "What does this mean about you?" he asked his reflection. His refection had no answer but looked content, so he went back to bed.

At ten the next morning, he woke up a third time when a hot, warm mouth landed on his. Apparently, whatever happened last night didn't need to be over. Tanner was stunned at how happy that made him.

When the kiss ended, Tanner asked, "Don't you have a girlfriend back home?"

Eli shrugged nonchalantly and answered, "I got a Dear John text from her two weeks ago. No great loss. She was sort of for show anyway."

Tanner furrowed his brow. "Why do you need someone for show? What's the big deal if you're gay?"

"Family obligations and expectations. They'll come around," Eli sighed. "Or not. And I'm bi anyway. I sometimes prefer men, and I'm incredibly attracted to you, Tan."

Chapter Five

For the next four years, Tanner and Eli remained roommates. Both were extremely popular guys who amassed
a large circle of friends to socialize with, and when they went
out, it was generally in a group. They both dated girls when a
date was called for—Tanner more than Eli—and were gentlemen with them. They kissed girls, but they never had sex with
them. Tanner sometimes felt as if he was searching for some
strange, illusive thing that he just kept trying and trying to
find and never could.

At night, however, Tanner and Eli fell into each other's
arms like long-lost lovers. They explored each other's bodies
in every way imaginable. Tanner learned how to fuck and be
fucked as a man. He learned that he loved the feel of Eli's
sculpted, muscular body beneath or over him as much as he'd
ever loved the feel of Zoë.

What confused him, however, was that he never once felt
any particular attraction to any other student on campus, male
or female. The girls were just a blip—a diversion. Other guys
never registered at all. He still pined for Zoë, but he also knew
he was in love with Eli.

Tanner also had another concern. He had political ambitions, but he wasn't blind to the fact that there were still
many, many people who would never accept a gay man in a
high political position. He would laugh to himself and wonder

if being bi-sexual counted. *Of course it does*. He couldn't lie to himself.

Right after their sexual relationship began, they made a pact that no one was to know. Eli pointed out sadly, "If you have political ambitions, you've seen over and over in the news how any little thing you've ever done can come back to haunt you. So, you need to be above reproach—no hint of a scandal. And between us, we have to look like best friends, period. No pet names, no fond looks at each other, that kind of thing. The bigots of the world can take anything and blow it up in your face." The pain in Eli's eyes was obvious as he continued, "*We* know it's not wrong, and someday it will be alright, but we're at the forefront of a huge change in society. It's still too soon."

Tanner laughed humorlessly. "Maybe I can make it to the White House and then come out."

"That's the spirit," Eli agreed. "You'll be a crusader for the LGBTQ community, but even then, you'll have haters. It would be a hard sell." He shook his head sadly and then brightened a bit. "Maybe by then the world will catch up and realize it's nothing to vilify. We can hope, right?"

***

Tanner always headed back to Honeybee Hollow at Christmas, and he made sure he went to church, volunteered at the soup kitchen and the animal shelter. He glad-handed and schmoozed with everyone in town, making certain he made a favorable public appearance. Several photos of "Honeybee Hollow's Princeton student" showed up in the town paper and website, showing just how handsome and civic-minded he was.

During spring break, he headed to the Hamptons with Eli and the rest of the Whittakers where he soaked up what it was like to live life as a blue-blood American aristocrat. He learned about life for the mega-wealthy and pumped Eli's parents constantly and politely for information. Tanner never pretended to be anything other than a young man from a small town in rural Kentucky, the son of a veterinarian and a librarian, but his brilliance was always evident in his inquisitive questions and thoughtful answers.

Eli's father was so taken with Tanner that he secured summer jobs for him each year in Washington, DC with a variety of his cronies. Tanner learned the inside ropes about politics and campaigning. He filled his head with tricks of the trade, so to speak. He was certain this information would prove invaluable to him as he advanced his career.

The only downside to his time with the Whittaker family was that Mrs. Whittaker seemed hell-bent on fixing Tanner up with Eli's younger sister Caroline. She was a lovely girl—as beautiful as her older brother, but Caro broke her mother's heart when she left college in her sophomore year to tour Europe with her boyfriend's rock band.

Tanner was extremely relieved.

Eli's interest lay in the marketing and promotional side of politics. He saw himself as a future kingmaker, and he knew just whom he wanted to promote to the highest job in the country. Tanner was remarkably good at making speeches and debating, where Eli preferred pulling strings.

As good things do, their blissful four years at Princeton all too soon came to an end. Tanner's plan was to go home to Honeybee Hollow and run for mayor. The former mayor had botched up so many things in the past few years, the climate for change was perfect. What they needed was a brilliant, attractive young go-getter. He knew the job was virtually his for the taking, and then he'd just have to bide his time until he could grab the job he really wanted—governor of the great commonwealth of Kentucky. He wouldn't be old enough for several years to put his hat in the ring, but being mayor would give him plenty of governing experience. Maybe he'd even put Honeybee Hollow on the map with his contributions.

Tanner had to accept, however, that there was no place for Eli in this scenario. Eli was heading back to New York where he'd work with his father.

"I can't believe this is over," he whispered into Eli's ear the night before graduation—the day they were to head back to their families and their real lives. "I'll always love you, Eli." Tanner lay his head on Eli's chest and heard the steady, comforting beat of Eli's heart.

Eli kissed the top of Tanner's head and whispered back, "I love you too, Tanner. Always. And it's not over. I promise I'll be there for you when you run for governor. And in the meantime, how about if we meet each other now and then and take a little vacation together?"

Tanner's head popped up and he looked into Eli's penetrating hazel eyes. "You think that will work? We could do that?"

"Sure. We'll just tell everyone we're going on a fishing trip." He snorted. Eli had never baited a hook in his life. "I'll tell everyone that my southern, country boy roommate from Princeton taught me how to fish, and it's my new favorite hobby. It's very relaxing, I hear."

"That sounds like heaven," Tanner said and kissed Eli.

"Also, don't forget we'll have the annual Princeton reunions. It would make perfect sense for old roommates to share a hotel room or an Airbnb," Eli pointed out with a grin.

Tanner smiled broadly. "Another great idea."

Changing the mood, Eli said in a serious voice, "Tan, I want you to consider something."

"What?"

Running his fingers through Tanner's silken hair, Eli asked, "That girl you've mentioned so many times... Zoë?" Tanner nodded. "I know you're still crazy about her, so go find her and marry her." Tanner leaned back and blinked at him in surprise as Eli continued, "It will be the best thing you can do for your career. You'll need a wife, not a husband, where you're going."

Tanner got a strange feeling in his gut when Tanner told him to marry Zoë. He'd actually fantasized about that very thing many, many times, but his loyalty to Eli had prevented him from ever taking the thought seriously. The reality of not having Eli in his life every day was excruciating, and he doubted a reconciliation with Zoe could ever happen whether he wanted it to or not.

"I fucked everything up with her. She probably won't give me the time of day," Tanner moaned. "And she shouldn't."

Snorting, Eli said, "You're resourceful; you'll figure it out."

"She's probably shacked up with some grad student at college right now and not available anyway."

"Work on it, Tan. There's not a grad student, or any man for that matter, who can hold a candle to you." He kissed Tanner's head once more.

"And what are you going to do, Eli?"

Eli gave a tiny huff. "I'm not the one with political ambitions. Maybe I'll just be a confirmed bachelor... or maybe I'll meet a woman who completely knocks my socks off. Who knows? She might be out there somewhere. You know there isn't anyone else I want to be with but you, Tan, but we'll just have to make do. Don't forget that you *need a wife*. A couple of kids wouldn't hurt either, future Mr. President."

Tanner's heart hurt with all the conflicting emotions he felt. "Eli, you know if I get married, I could never cheat on my wife to be with you. It would tear me apart to do that. And it would be the worst thing in the world to do to Zoë... or whomever I marry."

Smiling gently, Eli sighed, "I know, Tan. You're a good man. We still have a while, and we'll be able to see each other sometimes, but you see the big picture. Your ambition is very sexy."

He winked at Tanner. "If nothing else, we can always be best friends."

This time, Eli kissed Tanner on the mouth, and they spent the rest of their last night together making love. Neither had any idea how soon they'd be able to see each other again.

Chapter Six

Tanner returned to Honeybee Hollow a subdued man—but only inwardly. His need for Eli paralyzed him at night, and he couldn't sleep. Some days he wanted to forget all of his ambitions and drive straight through the night to get to Eli and marry the man. He also wanted to reconnect with Zoë and see if he had any hope of restoring anything with her. He was tormented by the thought of being without one of them for the rest of his life.

Several times he picked up his phone to connect with Zoë—but to say what? *I was a jerk and I'm sorry, so please take me back?* He doubted that would impress her.

During the day, Tanner smiled and networked and dazzled people with his charm. He made stirring, eloquent campaign speeches, sent out eye-catching flyers, and went door-to-door asking for support with humility and a firm handshake. People were taken in by his sincerity and his beautiful words. If there was a bit of sadness in his eyes, none of the townspeople noticed.

A few well-orchestrated calls from New York went to the proper media channels, and Tanner quietly and gradually became the darling of Kentucky. There was nothing over-the-top about his campaign, but everyone grew used to seeing images of the handsome, always smiling young man who'd set out to reform his hometown at the tender young age of twenty-two. His dedication was an inspiration.

When the election was called, he won eighty-five percent of the votes. His parents stood by him, so proud they could barely speak. Tanner was elated, but when he went home that night, all he could think to do was call Eli.

Pouring himself a bourbon and grabbing his phone, he crowed into it, "I did it, Eli. *We* did it. I took all of your advice, and now you'll have to call me Mr. Mayor!"

Tanner could hear the smile in Eli's voice when he answered, "I'm so proud of you, Tanner. Let me know if there's anything at all we can do to help you. You'll want to build a strong foundation for when you're ready to run for governor."

Tanner's successes as mayor of the small town became state news quite often. The media knew to keep tabs on the bright young star. They had all received polite suggestions in the form of advertising dollars to keep Mayor Lassiter visible and shown in a positive light at all times.

The wheels of the machine were beginning to turn.

***

Not too long after Tanner's victory, his sister Madison returned from Emory where she'd been studying business. Her personal life was in shambles, thanks to her asshole former boyfriend, which only strengthened her resolve to realize her dream of being a successful milliner.

Tanner saw her business aspirations as a great opportunity.

Right before Tanner took office as mayor, a factory that employed several of the Honeybee Hollow residents had folded. Bad business practices and expensive taxes had done in the owner, who fired everyone, locked the doors, and moved to Florida all in less than a week. It was a black time for the community.

While campaigning, Tanner promised tax reform to attract new businesses into the area, and he again picked Eli's dad's brain on how to accomplish that the best way. He worked out an anonymous deal through the Whittakers' foundation to secure a low-rate business loan for Madison so she could buy the necessary machines she'd need. All she knew was that it was a loan designed for female entrepreneurs. Tanner went in with her as a silent partner and bought the factory building, only his funding came from Eli.

The town watched the successful siblings flourish, and they could do no wrong. Tanner was the most popular mayor anyone could remember, and Madison's business grew exponentially as she made a killing with online sales. There were several trendy shops in New York that started buying her hats in large quantities. Again, she never knew that she had what amounted to a guardian angel taking care of her business from afar. Eventually, however, her designs became so popular, she barely needed any help from Eli.

Chapter Seven

Tanner tried dating some of the young women in Honeybee Hollow as well as the surrounding towns. Local residents constantly tried to set him up with their daughters, grand-daughters, nieces, or neighbors. Photos of him surfaced quite often with an attractive lady on his arm, but none of the women appeared more than once.

After three long years, Zoë finally returned to town. It took him six months of watching her turn away, walk away, ignore, and once even glare at him for him to finally show up at her doorstep with flowers in hand.

On a Thursday evening, Mayor Lassiter knocked on the door of Honeybee Hollow's beloved kindergarten teacher's house.

Zoë Deliban opened the door with a book in her hand. Bare-foot and wearing a pair of denim shorts that showed off her toned legs to perfection, she had on a tight tank top that didn't hide a bit of the contour of her pretty breasts. Her long brown hair was piled on top of her head in a random, oddly-shaped bun, and the expression on her face was not hospitable. Instead of stepping back and welcoming him inside, Zoë asked coolly, "Can I help you?"

Tanner immediately felt like a door-to-door salesman without a solicitation permit.

Mustering all of his courage and bravado, he held up the flower arrangement to her and asked, "Zoë, please, may I come in and talk to you? I won't take up a lot of your time. I'm sure you're busy."

"Why?"

"Why, what?" he stammered. "Why won't I take up your time, why should you let me in, or why do I think you're busy?"

"Any of those, Tanner. What are you doing here? You broke my heart years ago, and outside of one single lame-ass text message, you never contacted me again. And now you come with flowers like I'm something important to you? Wasn't your date last week with Felicia Bingham any good?" She hadn't meant for that last question to pop out of her mouth because it might have seemed she cared or paid attention, but somehow, she couldn't help herself.

Running his free hand through his hair, Tanner looked down and then straight into Zoë's eyes. "I have no idea how you know about Felicia, but believe me when I say I did that as a favor to my mother, and I have no intention of sitting through another evening of listening to her carry on about her pet chickens ever again." He let out an exasperated sigh. "Please, Zoë. Let me at least come in so no one sees me standing here looking like a pathetic loser."

"Yes, appearances are everything, aren't they? We wouldn't want the town to think you're anything but perfect now, would we?" She stepped back, and just as Tanner started to follow her inside, she closed the door in his face, nearly smacking his nose in the process.

Well, that could have gone better.

Chapter Eight

Not knowing what else to do or who else to call, Tanner phoned Eli. His friend sounded delighted to hear from him until he heard Tanner's voice.

"I fucked up again, Eli."

"Uh-oh. Tell me what you did."

Sighing, Tanner explained, "I went to see Zoë. She's done everything in her power to avoid me and act like I don't exist, which is pretty tough in a town the size of Honeybee Hollow, believe me. I finally just got fed up and bought a bouquet of flowers, went to her house, and got the door slammed in my face. So, now what?"

After a pause, Eli asked, "I guess the big question is, do you still have feelings for her?"

"You know I do, Eli. I have the same feelings for her as I do for you. And it's like my life is a big empty box of nothin' without you."

"Even with your exciting job as mayor?" Eli asked with a smile.

Tanner snorted. "The job is great. I love it, in fact, and I think I'm really doing some good things here for the town. But my personal life sucks! I'm so fucking lonely all the time, even though there are people around me constantly. Besides my family, I have my assistant Opal and the town council, and residents who ask me over to their houses for dinner so often, my oven probably has spider webs in it. But I have no one to... you know..." Tanner's voice dropped to a whisper, "love."

In a voice full of understanding, Eli said softly, "Look, Tanner. You knew this was going to be a challenge in many ways. You just have to play the long game. Start with small gestures and win back Zoë's trust somehow. Then up the ante gradually. Did she act really pissed at you?"

"You could say that. She told me I broke her heart and dumped her. She seems to think I'm either having a great time dating other women around town or if that's not working out well, I'm trying to get back into her good graces—like maybe she's some consolation prize or something." Tanner blew out an exasperated breath.

Eli brightened and exclaimed, "Tanner, that's great news for you!"

"How? She almost flattened my nose with her front door." Tanner rubbed his face thinking about it.

Chuckling, Eli explained, "Ignore the slamming door. It means she still cares, Tanner."

"You think so?"

"Absolutely. It kills me to say so because you know I love you and want you all to myself, but this is our *plan*, Tanner. Go get your girl. And call me when you've made some headway. Or... call me anytime. I know you'll eventually persuade her." Eli added in a voice choked with emotion, "You're irresistible."

So, bolstered by Eli's encouragement, Tanner ordered more flowers to be delivered to the kindergarten room. He added a card that said, "Always thinking of you. Love, T."

Zoë received the flowers, removed the card, and after school ended, she drove them to the local nursing home. She left instructions for them to be given to anyone who seemed particularly lonely that day.

The next week, another bouquet arrived with a card attached that said, "I'm an idiot, and I never stopped loving you."

She took those to the nursing home and dropped them off with the same instructions.

Week after wcck, the flowers arrived with notes that she removed. Each arrangement went to the nursing home, much to the delight of the residents who started to look forward to the weekly delivery.

Finally, after three months of flowers for which Zoë had never thanked Tanner or acknowledged in any way other than to get rid of them, a bouquet that was somewhat larger than the previous ones arrived. This time the note said, "Am I at least a little bit forgiven? Will you talk to me now? If so, please meet me at the park tonight at 8:00. Love, T."

***

Tanner arrived at the park at 7:30, he was so anxious to see Zoë. Unfortunately, it was a dreary, cold evening, and he sat on the bench shivering until 9:00. Alone. He finally gave up and went home when he feared he was losing feeling in his toes. *Why didn't I ask her to meet me somewhere indoors and warm like a restaurant or a bar? You know why, dummy. You wanted to avoid public humiliation.*

Tanner knew, through the town grapevine, that his flowers were gracing the rooms of the elderly folk at Coventry House rather than Zoë's classroom or house, but that was alright. Still, it was time to step up his efforts with the stubborn woman.

Soon it would be time for the annual Princeton reunions where he and Eli could put their heads together and come up with a plan. Tanner looked forward to it more than he could say.

Chapter Nine

As he'd done each year since graduation, Eli rented a huge suite in a local hotel for the reunion weekend. He made the trip to Newark via chauffeured limo to pick up Tanner at the airport. They greeted each other publicly with handshakes and bro hugs, but two hours later, once they checked into their suite for the weekend, they were all over each other. After a couple of hours of frantic, sweaty sex, they finally relaxed enough to have a conversation.

"You hungry?" Tanner asked. He'd had a much longer trip than Eli, and his stomach was beginning to rumble. He'd had to drive all the way up to Lexington to catch a flight to Newark. It had been a long-ass day.

Opening one eye, Eli conceded, "Yeah. You know they have that dinner tonight. Want to go or skip it?"

Rolling over to fondle Eli's taut abs, Tanner considered their options. "Would you rather just order some room service? I'm not sure I can even walk." He groaned a happy sound. "We can always see everyone tomorrow."

So, they ordered some giant steaks, scarfed their dinners down, and went back to bed. The king-sized bed was a particularly wonderful treat after their narrow dorm beds all during college. They spent hours tasting, fucking, clutching, stroking, and sometimes even biting—finally falling asleep wrapped around each other.

The next morning, they woke up too late to make it to the breakfast but wanted some fresh air, so they wandered out to the nearest Starbucks and filled up on breakfast sandwiches and tall coffees. Then they were too full to attend the luncheon, so they headed back to the hotel for more fun. They had both been starving for each other.

After a refreshing nap and shower, Eli asked, "So now what's your plan to woo the beautiful Zoë back into your good graces?"

Shaking his head slightly, Tanner answered with an exasperated sigh, "Hell if I know. The woman is so stubborn, she makes my blood boil. Sometimes I think she's just playing an evil game with me to see how far she can make me grovel, and other times it seems as though she's never going to come around. She did talk to me last week though, so that was encouraging. She even smiled. Well... sort of."

Eli brightened up and asked, "What did she say?"

With a bark of a laugh, Tanner said, "She came to a town council meeting about school funding, and she asked if taxes were going to go up or if teachers were going to be fired."

Eli grimaced. "Oh." He was thoughtful a while then and then spoke up, "Well, you're just going to have to up your game. Apparently, she's worried about money and worried about her job security, so we'll have to do something about that."

Sighing, Tanner explained, "I'm sure she still has student loans. She wasn't as lucky as Madison and I were in that department with Madison's full-ride to Emory and my free aid deal from Princeton." Eli nodded, and Tanner continued, "Zoë's dad owned a crappy little hardware store in town that he and his wife ran together. Right after Zoë came back to Honeybee Hollow, they sold out to a big chain store, took the profits, and bought a tricked-out old van that they moved into. They told Zoë she could have the house she'd grown up in—not that it's much of a prize. It's tiny and in pretty bad shape actually." He shook his head thinking of the peeling paint and the creaky door. "Anyway, then they said goodbye and took off to see the country. They'd never had a spare dollar to their name, and they'd never traveled, so this was a big thing for them. Honestly, I always got a kick out of them even though they're a couple of kooks." He let that sink in for a moment and then added, "Madison told me that Zoë kind of had a tough time when they left. It was like she was 'being abandoned again,' was how she put it to my sister. I assume the first time she felt abandoned was by me. Fuck, I feel like such a tool. No wonder she doesn't want to get near me again."

Looking every inch the businessman, Eli said, "Okay, Tanner. I have a plan."

They discussed it until it was time to get ready for the reunion dinner. It was with renewed hope that Tanner set out to greet and catch up with a bunch of their old friends.

Chapter Ten

A few weeks later, Zoë almost fainted when she got a letter in the mail announcing that her student loan was paid in full. She immediately called the number on the statement.

"Um, hi, this is Zoë Deliban, and I think there has been a mistake—not that it's bad, but I have a letter here saying my loan is all paid off...?"

The man on the other end of the call did some checking and came back sounding smiley. "Yes, Ms. Deliban. Thank you for your payment. The check arrived and it cleared just three days ago."

"I don't understand." Zoë frowned. "I didn't send a check like that."

"Well, I see that the bank account it came from was a new one, but it has your name on it," explained the man. "Thank you again. It's so nice to see someone pay up contentiously these days. So many people are defaulting on their loans. Please let us know if we can be of service to you for any future loan needs you have. Goodbye."

Zoë was left with dead air and a stunned expression. She didn't know what to think, so she immediately called them back and got someone else.

After explaining once again, she asked, "Can you tell me the bank the check was sent from as well as the account number, please?"

The lady on the phone answered, "I can tell you that the check was drawn from an account with Charles Schwab, but I can't reveal the account number without the proper ID from you."

Frowning, Zoë asked, "What kind of ID?"

"Your social security number and the account number from your bank."

"No, I *need* the account number!"

In a voice that sounded like someone talking to a dim four-year-old, the loan officer stated, "Ms. Deliban, I suggest you look at the checks they must have sent you from Charles Schwab. The account number is on the bottom of your checks."

"No, I... oh, never mind. Thank you." Zoë hung up.

***

Shortly after the student loan episode, Zoë received a similar letter congratulating her and thanking her for payment in full on the loan for her house. It had irked her no end that right before her parents took off on their journey, they'd taken out a mortgage, pocketed the cash, and left her to pay the bank back.

She made a call. "Hi, Mom. How are things on the road?"

"Zoë? Is that you?" Since Zoë was an only child, she wondered who else her mother thought it might be. This did not bode well for the conversation.

"Yes, Mom. Listen, I'll just cut to the chase. Did you and Dad just come into some money or something?" Zoë listened while her mother began to giggle uncontrollably.

Hiccupping and chirruping, her mother replied finally, "We sure did! We hit the casino in Reno... That has a nice ring to it doesn't it? Casino in Reno... A Reno casino!" She began to hum a little tune. "Your daddy hit the jackpot and it was in the casooni in Rooney." More giggles.

"I see, well I guess that explains things. Thank you from the bottom of my heart for taking care of things," Zoë said seriously. "It means a lot to me." This went a long way in Zoë's mind toward feeling more charitable toward her parents now that they'd stepped up like mature adults finally. At least in one respect.

"Uh-huh… we're taking care of the butterflies now. Is that you, Zoë?"

Zoë had a sneaking suspicion that her mother had partaken recently in either some magic mushrooms or some extra strong cannabis, and they weren't going to get much further with this conversation, so she said, "Be careful on the road, Mom. I miss you. Have fun. Bye now."

The last thing Zoë heard was her mother giggling. *At least she's happy.*

What Zoë did not know was that the jackpot her father had hit in Reno was a thousand-dollar win on the dollar slot machines. His winnings were gone in less than a day to things they could ingest, snort, and smoke.

Zoë couldn't deny that having the mortgage and the student loan paid made her feel a lot better about her life. She'd expected to be paying on those for years to come on a piddly little kindergarten teacher's salary.

So, she decided to put some needed repairs into her little house. She'd always found it curious that her parents ran a hardware store and never did any DIY repairs around the place. Perhaps they simply didn't care about it and were just marking their time until they could retire and have some fun. Anyway, she took a summer job giving swimming lessons again at the rec center and decided to put away every spare penny so she could fix up the house.

On a hot and sticky Friday evening late in June, she arrived home to find a crew of men loading up a truck in her driveway and getting ready to leave. She pulled up behind them, blocking them in and stormed out of her car.

"What's going on here? I didn't make any arrangements to have workers here today," she crabbed at them.

The four men, splattered head to toe with paint, all smiled at her, ignoring her angry words. One guy offered his hand and said, "It's been great doing business with you, Ms. Deliban. Looks beautiful, don't it?" He did a quarter turn toward her house and regarded it proudly. The house had been returned to its formerly beautiful appearance of brilliant white with cheerful blue trim. Zoë remembered it had looked like that when she was a little girl, and she'd always been delighted with her pretty house. Over the years, however, the blue trim had faded to blah and the white paint began to peel off of the wood siding. It made her sad to come home to that day in and day out.

Narrowing her eyes, she asked, "What do you mean 'doing business' with me? I didn't hire you, although," she softened her voice and turned to their work, "it looks like you guys did a fantastic job. The house looks amazing."

"The credit card payment cleared just a few minutes ago— as soon as we finished, the office ran it through. It's been a pleasure. Now, if you'll let us out, we can all get home to our families for supper."

"Oh, uh... right. Sorry." Zoë didn't have much choice other than to move her car, so she climbed back in and then rolled down her window asking, "Do you have a business card so I can call your office, please?"

"Sure, ma'am, but they just closed and won't back open again until Monday." He produced a card and handed it to her.

"Of course they won't," she chuckled. She backed her car away and waved as they drove off. Once she was parked in her garage, she picked the card up off the seat next to her, thinking it was face down. But when she flipped it over, she could see it was just blank white card stock on both sides.

What the...?

***

Tanner saw the changes in Zoë right away. She seemed to breathe easier and had a happier look on her face when he noticed her going about her business around town. She'd had her hair professionally styled, though it was still long and lovely, and she definitely had some new clothes. He especially loved catching sight of her wearing a light sundress that showed off her toned body.

Since it was summertime, and she wasn't teaching, Tanner didn't want to chance leaving flowers on her doorstep in the heat of the day, so he suspended his weekly deliveries for a while. He didn't like that one bit because he feared she would think he'd lost interest. So, on Friday evening a couple of weeks after her house was painted, he hopped in his car and headed to her house to see once more if she'd talk to him.

Oh, the sadness that ensued.

Tanner approached her house—which now had some pretty flowering pots lining the front walkway up to her door. His heart dropped out of his chest when he saw her walking toward a car in her driveway. She was smiling happily with her hand laced into the crook of a man's arm.

Who is that creep, and what is he doing with my woman? Tanner slowed down enough to grab his phone and snap a photo of the guy with Zoë, and it also took in the back of the guy's shiny sedan with his license plate showing. The guy looked vaguely familiar.

Zoë was so busy looking into the eyes of her date, she didn't see Tanner's car drive by. Her date was so busy leering at Zoë, he missed Tanner as well.

Tanner went home and poured himself way too much bourbon to drink on an empty stomach. After a couple of gulps, he stared at the golden liquid and the melting ice in his glass as he pondered the craptastic turn of events. Since he couldn't think of anything else to do, he called Eli.

His call went to voicemail. *Well, of course. Everyone has something better to do on a Friday night. Maybe I should ask Phoebe Sissman out. She's only a little cross-eyed.* Clearing his throat when he got to the beep at the end of Eli's request for him to leave a message, Tanner announced in a slurred voice, "Hey, Eli. I miss you, and now Zoë has a boyfriend. My life sucks. Bye."

Twenty minutes later he got a text.

Eli: Sorry man. I'm out on a date, but she just left to "powder her nose." Why do they say that? Women! Hang in there. Maybe she'll get sick of him. Or maybe it's time to look for someone else. My sis Caro broke up with the rockstar... interested? The clock is ticking. Gotta go.

Tanner was definitely not interested. He wanted one woman, and she was lost to him, apparently. *Maybe it's just one date though, and the guy has awful breath and a tiny dick. I can always hope.* The thought of anyone's dick, tiny or otherwise, getting near Zoë made him nearly tear up. He poured another bourbon and eventually fell asleep in his chair in front of a lousy movie.

On Saturday, Tanner invoked his mayoral privilege and traced the license of the car he'd seen Zoë getting into. It turned out it belonged to some jerk named Brandon Johnny. *Even his name sounds dumb.* Brandon had recently relocated to Honeybee Hollow to sell real estate. *So that's why he looks familiar. His face is on the shopping carts at the Piggly Wiggly. He has to be a douche; I just know it. What's she doing with that dipshit?*

Tanner wanted to kick himself in the ass. All of the improvements he'd made in Honeybee Hollow were definitely getting the town the recognition it deserved, and the local economy was beginning to thrive, but in doing so, it attracted the likes of Brandon Johnny who hoped to swoop in and make a killing selling houses and commercial properties.

Every time he saw that guy's photo, with his plastic smile and overly-styled hair, Tanner wanted to puke. He always threw something over the mini-poster on the shopping cart when he needed anything from Piggly Wiggly. Tanner didn't need to see, *"Your friend in the real estate business! Call Brandon Johnny to get the job done!"* each time he bought cereal.

Tanner saw Zoë and Brandon the Douche all over town. They ate out, they went to the movies and to community theater events. They volunteered together at all of the charitable places that Tanner had always considered "his." But the worst thing of all was that Brandon seemed hell-bent on becoming friends with Tanner. Tanner hated the asshole's guts—just because. But, as mayor, he couldn't be rude to anyone and get away with it.

Each time he saw them together, Tanner watched Zoë for any sign of unhappiness or discomfort, but all he could tell was that she put up with Brandon's fawning and seemed a teensy bit bored. Tanner remembered all too well what Zoë was like when she was passionate about something, and he didn't get a whiff of that from her now as she spoke to Brandon.

Brandon tried and tried to get chummy with Tanner, but so far Tanner had managed to avoid him pretty successfully. Not only did the guy piss Tanner off because he was with Zoë, but Tanner also suspected Brandon wanted to get in the good graces of the mayor for his own purposes that had nothing to do with friendship.

Even though Tanner had ducked Brandon's calls so far, his assistant answered the office phone one afternoon about a year after the couple had started dating. Opal put the call through to Tanner who answered distractedly. He'd been studying a proposal for some maintenance work for the nearby bridge that needed attention. The proposal was full of doubletalk and vague language that confused him, so he wasn't paying attention when he picked up the phone. "This is Mayor Lassiter."

"Tan, my man! Hi buddy!" a cheerful voice said too loudly in Tanner's ear.

"Sorry, who's this?" The voice was familiar, but he couldn't place it. He wondered if it was an old friend from college.

"It's Brandon, Tanner. Brandon Johnny. Zoë's boyfriend." Tanner felt his stomach lurch as the asshole carried on. "Me and Zoë were talkin' last night and I, uh...*we* decided we'd like to have you over for dinner at her place. I didn't realize you two knew each other so well. She said you kinda grew up together. Anyway, you're in for a treat. Zoë's pot roast is just as tasty as she is. Feel free to bring a date, if you like."

Tanner wanted to hurl. But maybe he'd learn something if he saw Brandon up close. He also couldn't resist the chance to be near Zoë, even if she had a stupid boyfriend. Then he brightened up when he realized Brandon had said 'her place' as if they weren't living together. *Thank heaven for small favors.*

So, that Saturday, Tanner got dressed up and arrived at Zoë's house right on time. He had a bottle of wine and a bouquet of flowers that he offered to Zoë when she answered the door.

Zoë's face was as red as he'd ever seen it. *Maybe she's been slaving over the hot stove? Or is she as uncomfortable as I am?* Just to test the waters a bit, Tanner leaned in and gave her a friendly peck on the cheek. "You look beautiful, Zoë. Thanks for having me." He looked around. "Where's Brandon?"

She hadn't pulled away, and he took that as a good sign.

Taking the flowers, Zoë answered in a shaky voice, "Thank you. Oh, um... he's late. I'm sorry. He called a couple of minutes ago and said he had to write up an offer. Some people who've been on the fence about a house now want it all of a sudden, and he couldn't put them off. Come in and have a drink, Tanner. He shouldn't be too long."

"The house looks amazing, Zoë." Tanner had to suppress a smile.

"Thanks." She got a faraway look on her face and continued, "It's so weird. The house had been looking pretty bad for quite a while, but then out of the blue someone had it painted for me. It might have been my parents, but that's not really their style. So, I think it was either the neighbors who got sick of looking at it or, more than likely, it was Brandon, and he wanted to surprise me. He hinted that it was his doing but he won't confirm it one way or the other. Anyway, it was sure a beautiful gesture."

Oh crap.

Tanner hated himself for asking but couldn't help it. "Are you guys serious?"

Handing Tanner a bourbon on ice, she looked put out. "It's not really your business, is it?"

Knowing he only had a short time alone with Zoë, Tanner decided to lay it all out for her. "Zoë, I still love you. I never stopped. I know how badly I messed up, but I was young and stupid, and I thought I was doing you a favor, especially when I saw the heartache Madison went through trying to maintain a long-distance relationship with her boyfriend during college. Please, can't you give me a chance?"

"Brandon asked me to marry him," she whispered, looking at her hands in her lap. She wasn't wearing an engagement ring at least.

"You can't be serious! Do you really love *him*?" Tanner bellowed.

Zoë looked pleadingly into Tanner's eyes. "I don't think he'd ever leave me."

"That's not an answer." Tanner took a gulp of his bourbon and shuddered. It was the cheap stuff. "Ugh! Why did you buy this shit?" he asked looking into the glass like it was the enemy.

"Oh, sorry. That's Brandon's favorite brand."

"Figures." Tanner set down the glass on a coaster and grasped Zoë's hand. Again, she did not pull away. "Zoë, I can see it written all over you. He's not the man for you. You know that's a fact."

Zoë's soulful brown eyes bore into Tanner's, and as a tear began to form in the corner of one eye, she answered, "Maybe not. But I think I'm going to tell him yes. Probably. Soon...maybe. He's a decent guy, Tanner. He wants kids. He'll move me into a bigger house. He'll... oh!" She snatched her hand away. "He's here."

The kitchen door lamed then and a voice shouted too loudly considering the size of the house, "Hey, babycakes! I'm home!"

Tanner whispered to her one last plea, "Don't do it Zoë. Please don't."

Brandon marched into the room, all smarmy smiles and looking sweaty. "Tan, my man! Good to see you! Hi, baby!" He leaned down and kissed Zoë. "Can we eat soon, ZoZo? I'm starved."

ZoZo? Oh. My. God. Tanner's stomach turned to acid, and he thought the cheap bourbon was about to make a second appearance. Putting his hand to his forehead, he realized he was getting a migraine.

Standing on unsteady legs, Tanner announced, "Zoë, Brandon, I'm afraid I'm going to have to take a raincheck on dinner. I'm suddenly feeling rather ill, I'm afraid. And, Brandon, it's Tanner—not Tan." *No one is allowed to call me that except Eli.* "I'll say good night to y'all now. I'm sorry." Without a backward glance, Tanner beat it out the front door and drove away.

He didn't want to go sit in his lonely house, and he didn't want to grab a drink at the Sundance Bar where he might have to talk to people, so he drove aimlessly around listening to music for an hour. Finally, when his stomach began to feel better, he called in an order to the Sock Hop for one of their great burgers, picked it up and went home to eat in solitude. Once he felt a little more human, he made a call.

"Eli, it's time to go fishing."

With no hesitation, Eli answered, "Okay. I know just the place. Drive up to Lexington on Friday, and I'll have the plane come pick you up. I'll text you the time when I get the schedule figured out."

Relaxing even more, knowing he'd see Eli, Tanner sighed happily. "Thanks man. You have no idea how badly I need you."

"I can't wait."

***

Tanner thought he would hear about a house sale closing shortly after his aborted dinner with Zoë and Brandon, but the sale must have fallen through. Nothing showed up.

Chapter Eleven

The next couple of years were brutal. Tanner ran into Brandon all over town. Brandon unfailingly tried to cozy up to Tanner and act as though they were longtime buddies. Because they were in public, Tanner had to keep his cheerful mayor face on and smiled at the guy with absolutely no sincerity whatsoever. And all the time, his insides seethed at the thought that Zoë could stand to be around the creep. *His* Zoë.

The only thing that kept Tanner feeling human during this brutal attack on his heart were the weekends he spent every couple of months with Eli. Each time they went fishing, it was to a different—and very remote—cabin that would be fully stocked for their convenience. Eli was the ultimate planner and organizer. They would arrive at some idyllic location where they spent the day fishing and the night making love. Eli became a decent fisherman and actually enjoyed it, and Tanner felt as if he could breathe in Eli's company. Being mayor was great, but it was also exhausting in a town that made your business everyone's business.

But in Honeybee Hollow, something slowly became apparent to Tanner as he observed Brandon go about his daily routine. The jerk seemed to act like he was incredibly busy all the time with his real estate sales, but Tanner saw very little evidence of properties actually changing hands. Once in a blue moon, a house sale would close, but certainly not at the rate that would make anyone rich as an agent.

Tanner managed to "bump into" Zoë now and then. Each time he asked her in an offhand, friendly way how life was going with Brandon. She always gave a similar answer. "He's working really hard, and things are fine." She still wasn't wearing a ring, and Tanner liked that a lot. Maybe he could play the long game after all.

Since Tanner was burning up with curiosity about what Brandon actually did all day, he finally hired a private investigator to check him out. It only took three weeks for the detective to furnish Tanner with enough evidence to bury the creep. Brandon wasn't breaking the law, but he was lying his ass off to Zoë. Armed with photos, Tanner now had a big decision to make. After stewing about it for another couple of weeks, he finally dialed her number.

He was gratified when Zoë answered his call cheerfully. "Tanner? Hi, how are you?"

She sounded good, and he hoped she wouldn't kill the messenger. This was not going to be easy. *Maybe I should have just left the photos in her mailbox anonymously.* Taking a fortifying breath, Tanner asked, "Zoë, do you think you could meet me somewhere? I have something really important to show you."

"What?"

"I think it's better if you see it before we discuss it. Can you come over to my place after school tomorrow maybe?" He didn't want her to be out in public in case she got really upset.

"Your place? Tanner, what is it?"

"Look, Zoë, it's something you really need to know about and I think you'll want to have some privacy."

In a no-nonsense voice, she asked, "Does this have to do with Brandon cheating?"

"Wh.. you *knew*?"

Sounding relieved, she answered, "Let's just say I suspected. Do you have some kind of proof?"

"I have photos, and they're pretty damning."

Much to Tanner's surprise, he heard Zoë burst out laughing. "Hallelujah! Tanner, are you home right now?"

"Uh... yeah."

"I'll be right over."

Chapter Twelve

Tanner couldn't believe his ears. He looked down at his wrinkled clothes and ran to grab a clean shirt at least. Thinking fast, he brushed his teeth and gargled some mouthwash to get rid of pizza breath. Then he dashed around his living room picking up random detritus like dirty plates, coffee cups and drink glasses. By the time he'd made two trips to the dishwasher to get rid of the evidence of bachelor living, he heard his doorbell ring. He and his house weren't perfect, but they'd have to do.

Tanner opened the door. And there she was. His Zoë. The most beautiful creature in the world. He just stood there admiring her before she broke his reverie by asking, "Tanner, may I please come it?"

Feeling like an ass, he stepped back stammering, "Oh, uh, sure. Sorry. Can I get you anything? Something to drink maybe?"

"Sure," she agreed. "I'll have whatever you're having." She looked around his living space and decided to take a seat on the couch. There was a large manila envelope sitting in the middle of the coffee table that drew her attention.

Tanner set down two glasses of sweet tea and sat beside her. Clearing his throat, he said, "Zoë, I hope you don't think I was somehow invading your private life, but I hired someone to check out what Brandon does all day long. He's such a blowhard about his business, but I know for sure that there isn't enough real estate changing hands in town to keep him as busy as he claims to be."

Leveling him with a look, Zoë answered, "It *is* an invasion, Tanner, but I would have hired someone too if I'd felt like I could afford it. So, I'm not as mad at you as I probably ought to be. I've spoken to Brandon about his so-called business meetings, but he's always been cagey and super defensive. I've even made some inquiries and found out investigators are too expensive for my teacher's salary. I thought of following him, but he'd have caught onto that in a hurry. So, I just waited for him to make a mistake. And now, apparently, you've done the dirty work. Show me what you have, please."

Tanner unclasped the envelope and pulled out a series of time-stamped photos. They were all taken from far away, and some were clearly blown up details taken from quite a distance. In each one, Brandon was with a woman. Three different locations and three different women. Among them, there was a group of shots of Brandon and a woman standing in the doorway of a house. In one of the photos, they were kissing, and it was not the kind of kiss you'd give a casual friend or relative. It was the full-on groping, "I can't get enough of you" kind of kiss. Both Brandon's and the woman's faces were recognizable in the shots where he'd turned to leave.

Another group showed Brandon checking into a cheap local motel. The most damning of the pictures was shot through the partially opened curtains of a ground floor room. It showed Brandon's bare butt with his pants pulled down. He was angled so that the shoulder of a woman with long blonde hair was just visible as she knelt in front of him. It was pretty obvious what she was doing, especially since Brandon's head was thrown back in apparent ecstasy. His face was clearly recognizable in semi-profile.

The last bunch was taken in the parking lot of the Piggly Wiggly at night. Brandon stood next to a car where the driver's door was open. He was nuzzling the neck of a woman who stood quite close to him with her hand grasping something between them. It was impossible to see exactly from the angle the shot was taken, but the assumption was that she had his dick in her hand. This suspicion was solidified when the next shot showed him turning away and tucking himself back into his pants. Classy!

"I bet each of the timestamps are from days he claimed to be closing a deal," Zoë mused dispassionately. "What a scumbag. Thank you, Tanner. May I have these?"

"They're all yours, Zoë. What will you do now?" He was too afraid to hope this gave him a chance with her.

Slipping the photos back into the envelope, she thought for a moment. "Well, first of all, I'm going to get rid of all of the crap he's strewn all over my house. Then I'll get the locks changed because I stupidly gave him a key. Then I guess I'll have to confront him again, only this time with proof."

Itching to run his fingers through her hair, Tanner asked, "Is there anything I can do to help?"

Her eyes flashed at him, and she blurted out, "I think you've done plenty already."

"Only because I didn't want you marrying that cheater. You know your happiness is very important to me, Zoë."

She looked down and admitted softly, "I wasn't going to marry him."

Jolting back a tiny bit, Tanner asked, "Then what were you doing with him for so long? Why waste your time on someone like that? I don't get it."

Zoë hung her head and said softly, "He was so nice and attentive at first. It was as if I could do no wrong. My ego had taken some pretty big hits, and I needed it." She raised her face and looked him in the eyes for a second, letting that sink in. "But I could never make myself fall in love with him. He just never felt right. Still, it was nice to get out and have someone to do things with. The more he asked to move in, or have me move in with him, the more I pulled back. And then he asked me to marry him, and I told him I wasn't ready. That's when he started showing up late, and sometimes, he'd smell faintly of perfume or he'd be too tired to... you know..."

"Please," Tanner put up a warning hand, "don't go into details for me. I get it."

"It wasn't often at first. And it was just a feeling I got, but in the past few months, it's become more of a pattern. I actually asked him about it just a few days ago, and he got really angry with me. He promised me he loved me more than anything, and he'd never, ever do such a thing."

Tanner waited to see if the tears would come, but Zoë either wouldn't cry in front of him or she truly was resigned to a life without the cheater. He longed to take her hand and offer her his love. It was too soon, even if she was over the jerk—he knew that. Nevertheless, he told her softly, "Zoë, you are the most perfect woman I've ever met. I want to be something more to you than an old friend or an ex. I won't pressure you, but please... I would so much love to have a second chance with you."

Looking at her hands resting in her lap on top of the envelope, she chewed her lip for a moment. Finally, she looked up and told him, "I'll think about it."

Letting out a relieved breath, Tanner said, "Alright. That's more than I could hope for. I know I hurt you, Zoë, and I'd love to spend the rest of my life proving to you that I'll never do it again. I'm not an eighteen-year-old who's full of himself anymore." He finally reached for her hand and clasped it.

Zoë snorted, "No, you're a twenty-eight, almost twenty-nine-year-old who's full of himself. I know about all of your political ambitions, Tanner. Your sister's my best friend, remember?" She looked at her hand in his. "Frankly, that's another thing to come to grips with. I'm not sure I'm cut out for a life in politics."

A wide grin split Tanner's face. "Well, it's good to know you've at least thought about me and what kind of a future we could have together."

"Don't get ahead of yourself, Tanner. I said I'd *think* about it. That's all." She pulled her hand loose. "I better go. There are some things I need to do."

***

When a woman says she has "things to do," men better pay attention, Tanner knew. But he had no idea the lengths Zoë would go to.

The next morning, he was out of cereal so he decided to make quick a run to the Piggly Wiggly for a carton of eggs and some cream for his coffee. Even though it was early, there was a crowd of people standing in the parking lot talking animatedly and laughing their heads off. Each of them had a shopping cart they were staring at and guffawing about. Tanner couldn't stand the suspense, so he exited his car quickly and approached the crowd.

Noticing Tanner's approach, one of the men who served on the town council hollered, "Mayor Lassiter! You've got to see this!" He turned his shopping cart around so that the small poster inside was visible to Tanner. "He's definitely 'getting the job done' here," the councilman snorted.

Where the annoying, grinning photo of Brandon had been, now the photo of him with his pants down and his bare butt showing had been glued over the top.

My God, I love that woman.

***

Less than a week later, Brandon Johnny, who was now a town legend, crawled back into the hole from whence he'd come and no one in Honeybee Hollow ever saw him or heard from him again. Hereafter, if anyone ever referred to him at all, it was by calling him BJ.

Chapter Thirteen

Zoë was planning to spend Thanksgiving Day working in the local food pantry since her parents were living it up in San Francisco and weren't planning to make the trip home.

The Lassiters had planned to celebrate the weekend before Thanksgiving because Madison needed to get back to her millinery shop in Louisville to work on Black Friday. So, Madison was in town with her boyfriend Halden Dahl, and they stopped by to see Zoë that Sunday. It was then that they roped her into having dinner with the whole family back at Madison and Tanner's parents' house.

After reluctantly agreeing to join them, Zoë was afraid she still wasn't yet ready to see Tanner. She knew what he wanted from her was to rekindle their relationship, but there was just so much at stake.

Dinner was comfortable, at least for a while. Halden had plenty of entertaining stories to tell, and the Lassiters asked Tanner a few pointed questions about his gubernatorial campaign. Zoë knew it was only in the early stages. The election was still a year away, but the groundwork was beginning to be laid.

Mrs. Lassiter had naturally seated Zoë next to Tanner at the table, and toward the end of the meal she looked around the table making the observation, "This is almost like when you were all high school kids, except Madison's boyfriend Crunch —or Kevin, if you will—used to sit where you are, Halden." She frowned a little and went on, "I'm sorry to say, I never liked that boy very much. Halden, dear, you are a vast improvement." Then she smiled at Zoë and Tanner. "And I never could understand why the two of you didn't continue your romance after high school. You were as cute together as can be."

Zoë's face went red and Tanner spluttered, "How did you know Zoë and I had a romance?"

"Tanner, I'm your mother," she laughed. "There isn't much that gets by me, and it was pretty obvious when you took her to your senior prom. But more than that, how many other girls are there in town with hair like Zoë's? None I can think of. And I used to find evidence of it rather often in your bed when I changed the sheets."

Zoë gasped.

Madison giggled.

Tanner looked embarrassed.

Dr. Lassiter asked Halden, "Care for another roll, son?"

"Don't mind if I do, sir," Halden answered with a smile.

"So?" asked Mrs. Lassiter. "Is there any hope of rekindling the spark with the two of you?" When they both just gaped at her, she sighed as if to herself, "Just think of the beautiful babies..." Without waiting for any response, she stood and announced, "I'll just go put on the coffee. Does everyone want pecan or pumpkin pie?" She looked fondly at Halden. "Or both?"

Dr. and Mrs. Lassiter had always been pretty accepting of what went on, and Zoë decided she needn't worry about their high school dalliances. There had been no judgment in Mrs. Lassiter's statement—only hope. So, when Tanner drove her back to her place, she found herself relaxing a little where he was concerned. Maybe he *had* matured and wouldn't hurt her again. They were both adults now, she reasoned. Still—he had those ambitions of his and she certainly didn't want to be his downfall.

***

It was a short drive—only a few blocks, and they could have walked if the temperature hadn't been so frigid. It was unseasonably cold for fall. Neither seemed to know what to say, however, so it was a silent few blocks.

Tanner pulled up into Zoë's driveway, and she turned to him, regarding him with a steady gaze. He looked at her hopefully, so she asked, "Would you like to come in for a drink?"

Yesss! "Sure, that sounds nice. Thanks, Zoë." *Progress at last!*

Unfortunately, when they got inside, the temperature wasn't any better than it had been outdoors. "Oh no!" Zoë muttered. "The stupid pilot light must have gone out again on the furnace. Have a seat, Tanner, and I'll go try to fix it."

Feeling chivalrous, Tanner argued, "I'll do it. You just fix us some drinks and I'll be right back. Oh, do you have matches?"

"This happens so often with that crappy old piece of garbage, there's a long-necked grill lighter downstairs on the shelf. You'll see it. It's red."

A couple of minutes later, Tanner returned, and the sound of forced air could be heard rattling through the ducts. It was still cold, though. Tanner took a seat a few inches from Zoë on the couch and eyed the glass of golden liquid she'd poured for him and set on the coffee table. "Is that...?"

Zoë interrupted his question with a chuckle. "Don't worry. It's not that rotgut Brandon drank. I bought a bottle of the good stuff the other day for... uh..." Her voice trailed off and Tanner scooted a couple of inches closer with a smug grin.

"Are you too cold?" he asked. She nodded and he could see her shivering slightly. "Can I help?" Feeling smooth, he scooted closer still so they were touching and he put his arm around her shoulders. "Here you go; I'll warm you up. He tucked her head under his chin. His jacket was open, so his body heat invaded Zoë immediately. "This is nice, Zoë. You feel so good in my arms." He leaned his cheek on her head, feeling her silky hair. It felt like home, and he knew he hadn't breathed so easily in years.

They sat that way for several minutes, just soaking up the feel of each other, when Zoë finally spoke up. "Tanner?"

"Hmm?"

"Can we... um... can we maybe try it out... and take things slowly?"

Tanner felt his heartbeat accelerate as he pulled back to look at her. "Oh Zoë. Slowly, quickly, whatever you want. I want to be here for you. I'll try not to come on too strong, so let me know if I get ahead of myself, okay? I don't ever, *ever* want to hurt you."

"Alright. Now don't go getting any ideas here, Romeo. I'm just going to take off my jacket because you're such a heater, I'm starting to get too hot." She stood and started to go hang her jacket in the hall closet. "Want me to hang yours up too?" Tanner whipped his off as well and handed it to her.

Once Zoë sat back down next to him, Tanner couldn't stop himself. He leaned in to kiss her. Softly at first, and as she relaxed, he pressed his tongue to her lips. She slowly opened to him, and he greedily invaded her. She tasted like heaven. Like his Zoë.

Eventually gaining the perspective he sorely needed, Tanner pulled back and took a deep breath. "My mama is right, you know. We were excellent together. We can be again."

Clasping both of Tanner's hands Zoë looked at him seriously. "Do you really think I'm a suitable woman to be with you in the long run? I know I'm getting way ahead of myself by asking this, but it needs to be said. Do you really think I'm fit to be a governor's wife? Why do you think I've been working so hard at avoiding you? I'm a nobody."

"Never say such a thing about yourself. Everyone loves you. I love you! I've watched you for years around town moving with grace and your beautiful manners—well, except for the blow-job posters at the Piggly Wiggly."

Fluttering her eyelashes at him, she asked in a falsely coy voice, "Whatever do you mean? You think I had something to do with that?"

Tanner snorted.

Skewering him with a look, she asked plaintively, "Seriously, my parents are vagabonds who are basically born-again hippies. Wouldn't they embarrass you?"

"Your parents are just, um..." he hedged, "colorful! And besides, everyone has skeletons in their closets. Did Madison ever tell you the story of how our name changed from Ascot to Lassiter?"

Furrowing her brow, she answered, "No. How does a name change? Did someone immigrate or something?"

"Hah! No. Our daddy's kin come from the southern Appalachian Mountains. His great-grandfather Thomas L. Ascot was a scoundrel and a moonshiner." Zoë noticed that Tanner's southern accent became more pronounced the more he got into his story. He'd lost a bit of it while he'd been away during his four years at Princeton, but it was back with a vengeance now.

Tanner continued, "He and his neighbor Wayne Dooley used to get into feuds all the time and steal from each other. One day, Wayne got so mad watching Thomas running away with a jug of moonshine, he shot Thomas in the ass with a shotgun. Everyone in the area could hear Thomas yelling, 'Oh, my ass! It hurts! My ass, it hurts!' So, from that day forth, everyone called him Thomas Assithurts instead of Ascot. Then one day, a tax collector came around, and asked who owned the still next to Wayne's property. Wayne, who was drunk and didn't want to pay any extra taxes, slurred, 'That's ol' Assithurts' property. He's prob'ly still off somewheres pickin' buckshot outta his butt.' The taxman misunderstood ol' Assithurts and wrote down Lassiter. So, the land became the property of the Lassiters."

"Tanner Lassiter, that is the most hair-brained story I've ever heard. You made that up," Zoë laughed.

"Oh, no. True story. Just ask my daddy. And you can ask my uncle; he owns a large distillery. Claims this is how the family business was founded." With a twinkle in his eye, he smiled and kissed her again. "I could stay here all night and kiss your face off, but I think it's time for me to go home. Thank you for the wonderful time and the fine Kentucky bourbon." He took one last swallow and asked, "May I take you out on a proper date next weekend? I know you have four days off because of Thanksgiving."

"Yes, I'd like that. What do you have in mind?"

Tanner gave her a thoughtful look. "Well, since I had no idea tonight would go this well, I haven't given it any thought. Can I see what I can come up with and get back to you?"

"That sounds good."

After a few more kisses, Tanner took himself home. He truly had not been this euphoric in years.

The knowledge that she'd been avoiding him for what she considered his own good made his heart hurt, so he promised himself to make it clear to Zoë that she was more than worthy. She was the most important person to him.

Then he thought of Eli and hoped he wasn't lying to himself. The idea that he'd have to give up having Eli as a lover just about killed him. Eli was always so steadfast in his devotion to Tanner—always thinking of what was best for him. If that wasn't true love, Tanner didn't know what was. Cutting Eli out might be like cutting off his right hand.

Chapter Fourteen

Since Honeybee Hollow had limited nightlife, they ended up driving over to Middlesex where they had an exquisite dinner in a rather incongruously located Moroccan restaurant. They laughed and felt self-conscious at first about eating with their hands, but quickly they got used to it. Feeling like having some fun, they began to feed each other bites of food.

The next day, photos of them surfaced all over the internet and the major caption read:

> Who is this stunning mystery woman who has stolen the heart of Mayor Tanner Lassiter, Kentucky's most eligible bachelor and the youngest entry in the Kentucky gubernatorial race? That sound you hear is the weeping from hundreds of southern belles who may have lost their chance to snag the handsome politician. The two lovebirds were caught canoodling after dessert in this romantic Middlesex, KY restaurant. Sorry, ladies! Dum-dum-dee-dum! Will there be a June wedding?

Courtesy of several friends who sent the story to her, Zoë was mortified. "Who writes like this, and who wants their photo plastered everywhere stuffing food in their mouth?" she asked Tanner.

In a soothing voice, Tanner countered, "It's fine, Zoë. Look how beautiful you look in the pictures. There's not one bad thing in the article. Relax."

Sighing, she relaxed. "I guess not. I wonder how long before my name's everywhere, too, and I'm not your 'mystery woman.'"

Laughing, Tanner asked, "So... June wedding? Shall we make them happy?"

"Tanner! What happened to slow?

"Slow went out the window when we got back from Middle-sex and you jumped my bones, Miss Deliban!"

Zoë laughed, "I blame it on the figs."

"Figs?"

"Yes, figs. Dolly Gunn has a chapter about natural aphro-disiacs, and figs are mentioned prominently. Therefore, I was under the influence of a substance I could not control because you took me out for Moroccan food." She tried, and failed, to look haughty, but Tanner grabbed her and kissed the daylights out of her.

"Let's go back to bed. I'm tired," Tanner said with a yawn. "Someone kept me up all night ravishing me."

"I can't. Sorry." She pulled away giggling as he nuzzled her neck.

Against her neck he grumbled, "Why not?"

"Because I have a birthday cake to make."

"You remembered?" Tanner blinked at her as she smiled shyly at him and nodded. "Thank you, but you don't need to bake. My parents have a birthday dinner planned for me to-night, so we can show up *together* and make them happy. If we told them we're getting married, it would make them ecstatic." He looked at her expectantly.

Frowning confusedly at him, Zoë asked, "What's the rush, Tanner? We've been back together for about a minute, and you want to get married? Can't we just get reacquainted for a while?"

"Zoë, I've told you I never stopped loving you, and I mean that. You're the only woman for me. Always."

She stared at him quizzically for a moment. "Didn't you date any girls in college?"

"Just now and then. I can't say I was celibate, but I never had a girlfriend. I knew right away that I'd messed up horribly, and I could never get interested enough in any of the girls at Princeton to pursue a relationship. It was always you I wanted to get back to." He reached up and stroked her cheek.

"Tanner, I'm sorry, but that sounds borderline weird. You broke up with me, remember? You were so sure we both needed to meet other people..."

"Well, what about you? Did you date any guys in college?" Tanner braced himself for an answer he didn't know if he wanted to hear.

"Um... well... not really. I mean, I did go out on dates and I had guy friends. I did stuff with groups, but I guess Brandon was the only real boyfriend I've had since you." She gave a little shudder.

Tanner snorted, "We saw how well that worked out." He noted her expression and quickly added, "I don't hold anything against you about that, Zoë, really. I can understand why you didn't want me to hurt you again—not that I would—and I can also understand how you wanted to have someone around who cared for you. I'm just really, really glad it didn't go any further with that asshole."

"Yeah, well... I am too," she said softly. Then she snuggled up to him. "Tanner?"

"Hmm?"

"I guess I'm not going to be baking today, so we better find something else to pass the time." She stood and took his hand, leading him to her bedroom. "This is so different from when we were younger. I was always so worried one of your parents would show up unexpectedly."

Tanner threw back his head and guffawed. "Zoë, either one of my parents would have just said something like, 'Be sure you're using protection!' and they'd have left it like that." He started pulling off his clothes as he spoke. "Honestly, I think everyone has always known you and I belong together. I was just too young and stupid to realize what I had, and you were too hurt by me being stupid. We have a second chance, Zoë." He was now naked and started working on removing her clothes. "So now, I'm going to show you," his voice went low and gravelly, "how deeply I love you and how you need to be married to me."

Tanner sat Zoë down on the edge of the bed and leaned down to kiss her deeply. He moved his lips down her neck and played with first one nipple and then the other with his lips and his teeth. Zoë sucked in a startled breath as he clamped down on one nipple and flicked it with his tongue. At the same time, his hand plunged into her pussy and he impaled her with a long finger.

She clamped her legs together, barely able to breathe, as he began thrusting in and out and then added a second finger. "Zoë honey, you're positively drenched for me. God, that's so sexy." Tanner dropped to his knees and spread her legs apart. He kept massaging in and out of her as he bent down to latch onto her clit with his mouth. Zoë cried out as he sucked it into his mouth the way he'd done to her nipple, using his firm tongue to drive her wild. Faster and faster his fingers plunged in and out, as he kept licking and sucking.

After only a few minutes, Zoë cried out, shaking with spasms. "God, Tanner, I love you!" she almost hiccupped.

Tanner reached for the bedside drawer and pulled it open. At the same time he asked, "Do you have any condoms? I just remembered I'm all out." Peering into the drawer, his eyes went round and he chuckled, "Well, well! Look who I found." He pulled out a brand-new box of condoms and a somewhat flexible, vibrating dildo. "It's BOB!"

Zoë scooted back and buried her face in her pillow. He could hear her groan, "I'm so embarrassed! And you're a big snoop."

Tanner, who was absolutely ready for action, ripped open a condom, put it on and announced, "There's nothing to be embarrassed about. This could be fun! These condoms are a little small though, so we'll need to be careful and not break this one."

Zoë pulled the pillow away from her face and stared at Tanner, who had his erection in one hand, and was brandishing her toy in the other. She gaped at him. "That doesn't bother you?"

"Why should it? It looks like a great idea to me. Open up your legs and get that horrified look off your face. I want to see how this could work." He located the button on the base of the vibrator and turned it on. "Hmm. Nice. Come on, honey. Open your legs for me."

Zoë finally complied, and Tanner positioned himself over her. He located her clit, and as he touched her with the vibrating toy, she gave an involuntary jump and a squeak. Tanner laughed softly, "I guess that means I found the magic button." Slowly he stroked her with the toy as she writhed.

"Tanner, I *need* you. Fuck me now, please!" She opened her legs even wider for him as he settled into place.

Sliding into her warm body, Tanner hummed his appreciation. "So good, Zoë. You feel like home and where I need to be." He watched with satisfaction as another orgasm cascaded through her. Slowly, he pumped in and out as she clamped and released him with her spasms. When she finally calmed, he asked, "Are you ready for something different?"

Opening her eyes, Zoë looked at him quizzically. "Different? How different?" Tanner watched as her pupils dilated, and he took this as a good sign. All the time, he kept up a steady in and out and felt his excitement building.

"Something else we can do with your toy. Do you have any lube?"

Zoë's mouth dropped a little, and she looked even more excited as she nodded. "Look in the cabinet under the drawer."

Tanner slowly and carefully pulled out and scooted over to look in the cabinet. He knew from personal experience that the lube he found was the good stuff, but the bottle was still sealed. "Have you ever used this stuff, Zoë?"

Shaking her head, she looked down shyly and mumbled, "Huh-uh. I just got it. The vibrator too, actually. Since I *thought* I was going to be on my own a while... I uh... got curious about some stuff I'd read and... um..."

"No need to explain. I'm just glad you never used this stuff with ol' BJ." This brought a round of giggles out of Zoë. "Were the dinky condoms his?"

"Oh, no. I actually bought those at the same time as I bought the good bourbon for you, and I didn't think to buy anything larger than what he used—even though I should have remembered. Sorry. I always made him wear one. I'm on the pill, but I never trusted him. Then when you showed me those photos, I thanked my lucky stars I'd been so adamant about it."

Tanner leaned in to kiss her and said, "And that's the last time he needs to ever come up. He no longer exists, okay?"

Smiling sweetly, she answered, "Fine by me. I've already forgotten him."

"It's nice to know that when you said you'd think about us getting back together you thought out some things pretty specifically—like condoms and good booze," Tanner laughed.

"Yeah. I know you can be persuasive, and I also knew it was just a matter of time before I agreed to see you again." Tanner beamed at her as she confessed this. "But, Tanner?"

"Hmm?"

"I guess you don't really need to use the condoms unless you want to. I'll leave it up to you. I know you'd never cheat on me."

Tanner's expression melted. "You have wonderful faith in me, Zoë." And then he whipped off the condom with a gleeful leer. "I've never had sex with anyone without using a condom, so this will be a first." Thinking briefly about how he and Eli had been religious about using them, he ditched the condom in the wastebasket and snuggled back up to her. "Are you ready for something interesting now?" She nodded eagerly so he flipped her over and raised her bottom up in the air. "Are you comfortable enough in this position, Zoë?"

"Yes, but it's kind of embarrassing having you staring at my naked butt."

"Oh, no reason to be embarrassed. You have a gorgeous ass. And now we're going to have some fun with it, okay?"

"I have a confession to make," Zoë announced solemnly.

Rubbing his hand over her soft as silk buttock, Tanner answered, "Something naughty or something bad?" Then he gave her a playful pat.

Zoë's voice was s bit muffled in the pillow. "Remember the time when we were at your house, and you fucked me while you fingered my butt?"

Tanner sighed happily, "That was a great day. I'd never seen you so turned on."

"That experience has been my go-to memory for years whenever I, um... need some extra mental stimulation."

"Well, well, honey," he chuckled. "That's quite a confession. So, now that we're grown-ups and all, let's see if we can improve on that memory, shall we?" Tanner trickled some lube into her butt crack and began to massage her hole gently. A couple more times, he added more lube and then gradually began to press his index finger inside ever so slowly. Zoë gave an encouraging moan, and he twisted and prodded. Then he stopped for a moment and fumbled around a bit. Zoë heard the crinkle of another condom wrapper. She looked back at him and was surprised to see him rolling it onto the thin, vibrating dildo instead of on himself.

"Oh! That's a good idea," she exclaimed. "Easier clean-up." Then she wiggled her butt that was still up in the air.

"Ready?" he asked.

"We'll see!"

Softly, Tanner crooned at her, "Just stay relaxed. I think you're really going to enjoy this." He smoothed even more lube onto the toy and turned it on. Then very carefully he eased it into her butt as she made encouraging noises. He kept the lube handy in one hand and squirted a bit more as he slowly drew the vibrator out and then back in. "Feel good, Zoë? You can't believe how sexy this looks from my angle. You're so perfect."

Zoë moaned and moaned with the feeling of the invading toy. And then Tanner did what she'd dreamed about for years, he shoved his dick into her pussy with a groan and Zoe cried out, "Yes! Oh, yes!"

"Fuck, this feels amazing! I don't know how long I'm going to last, Zoë. I've never been bare before and I can feel the vibrations. Between your hot pussy and the... oh God! Can you come this way?" He reached the hand that wasn't operating the toy around to her front and began to stroke her clit with his long fingers.

Zoë shook and pushed forward and backward in a complete frenzy of sensation, crying, "Oh God, Tanner. Oh... *oh...* I'm going to come *again!*" And she did.

Complete sensory overload drove through Tanner like a freight train. He knew in the very depths of his soul that he was irrevocably in love with this woman and had to get her to agree to marry him soon. She was his, damn it! His climax was so strong and intense, he practically screamed.

Ever so carefully, Tanner removed the vibrator and reached for a tissue to wipe up all of the lube. His spent dick slid out, and it was then he realized he needed more tissues. "Wow, things get a little messy without a rubber," he commented as he watched his seed dribble down the inside of her thigh. He felt like a Neanderthal when he realized the sight turned him on. Tossing all of the tissues into the wastebasket and setting the toy aside, Tanner encouraged Zoë to stretch out in bed so he could cuddle and spoon her from behind. Then he whispered into her ear, "I love you so much."

Zoë grabbed the hand that he snaked around her middle as she said, "I love you too, Tanner. And... you did it! You made it even better this time. That was amazing."

Chapter Fifteen

Tanner wasn't fooling around when he'd said he wanted to get married. During the weeks leading up to Christmas, he looked at rings and thought of the most romantic thing he could do to persuade Zoë to marry him. He was happier than he'd been since Princeton with Eli.

Tanner's conversation with his best friend had been bittersweet, however.

He waited until the evening, when Eli was likely to be home and alone. Zoë was Christmas shopping with a friend, so he had some time to himself. He poured himself a drink and got comfortable, but then he realized his hands were shaking when he made the call.

"Hey, Tan! I haven't heard from you for a few days. How's it going?" Eli's happiness in hearing from Tanner was obvious.

With a partially forced smile in his voice and a lump in his throat, Tanner answered, "Things are great, Eli. Really great. But..." *Oh crap. This is going to be hard.* "I, um... well, I finally got back together with Zoë. Can you believe it? You always said I'd be able to do it." Now he felt like he was rambling. "I used your advice again, and it worked." Tanner finally stopped making happy-sounding remarks and waited for Eli's reply. Instead, there was silence. "Eli? Are you there? Say something."

Eli finally cleared his throat and with a choked voice, he sounded like he was mustering up some enthusiasm for his soft reply. "I'm happy for you, Tan. I know that's what you've wanted all along. So... now it's done."

Tanner didn't have to guess that there was a double meaning to Eli's statement.

Done.

There would be no more fishing trips, no more sharing a room at reunions, no Tanner and Eli as lovers. Only Tanner and Eli as buddies. As much as that hurt, he'd have to live with it. It was their great plan, and it would help his chances of becoming governor. *Damned ambition!*

"God, Eli. This is hard," he said in a hoarse whisper. "I really do love Zoë. She's wonderful. But I love you as well."

Eli sighed and answered, "I love you too. But your campaign is going to have to really kick it up after the first of the year, so it's going to be important that everyone knows you're settling down. You were a little bit of a wildcard being so young and single. Well... single as far as everyone else knew. I knew you were mine."

A tear rolled down Tanner's cheek as he said, "Don't put that in past tense. Please."

"I have to! It's high time I found someone to settle down with too." Eli sounded sadly determined. "This hurts like hell, but we knew, and we hoped, it was coming. You're going to make an excellent governor. Just look at what you've done with that town of yours. It's listed on a bunch of blogs now on those Hidden Gems lists for little-known places that are great to live."

Tanner snorted, "That was your doing. You're the one with the press in your pocket."

"True enough, but your success as mayor has done a lot for the place, and if it hadn't, no one would write about it no matter what. I'm so proud of you and your accomplishments." Eli paused. "I wish I could kiss you right now... just one last time."

"Eli, are we even doing the right thing?" Tanner asked in a strangled voice. "Maybe I ought to come out to the world and just let everyone know I'm bisexual, and they can like it or... fuck them!"

"Come on, Tan. We've talked about this. Maybe by the time you're old enough to run for president, all the bigots will have died off or crawled back into their nasty little caves, but until we're sure of that, we can't take the chance." Eli shook his head, even though Tanner couldn't see him. "This is going hurt for a while, but you have Zoë in your corner now. You haven't told her about us, have you?"

"I have not. And frankly," Tanner muttered, "it's killing me to keep it from her. It feels like a sin of omission. I don't like lying. And you're wrong, for once, Eli. It's not gonna hurt for a while. I don't think I'll ever get over this kind of hurt. Just think of how miserable I was without Zoë. I had you, and I still felt incomplete. I don't mean to minimize my love for you in any way, Eli. I just feel sometimes like I need you both. Somehow."

"I get it. I do, Tanner." Eli sounded like he was taking a drink if the clinking of ice cubes were an indication. "I guess I'll see you after the new year. We'll kick up the campaign then. Are you going to get married soon?"

"We will if I have anything to say about it. The sooner the better. Zoë knows I'll have to be traveling around the state pretty soon in order to make a bunch of public appearances and speeches." Tanner seemed to brighten a bit talking about this. "It's not like she has a big family to worry about for a fancy wedding. If her parents even bothered to show up, it would be a miracle. Anyway, we'll see. I still need to pop the question."

"She'll say yes. You're irresistible, Tan." Eli let out a strangled sigh. "I'd say yes if you were asking me, but we know that's not happening."

"No. Sadly, it's not." Tanner paused. "God, listen to me! I should be happy about Zoë. It's not like she's some consolation prize or something. Now I just have to figure out when and how to propose. I was thinking Christmas, but that seems too trite somehow—offering her a ring for a Christmas present. I want our engagement and giving her a ring to be special and separate, you know?"

"You'll figure it out. I have faith in you."

Tanner blurted out, "Will you be my best man, Eli? Is that too much to ask of you?"

With a sad chuckle, Eli answered, "I'd do anything for you. Even if it means breaking my heart to do it." He took a deep breath. "Just let me know when and where to show up—if I'm not already down there overseeing your campaign. We'll get it done, Tan. Maybe I'll meet some beautiful southern belle in Kentucky and fall head over heels for her. You never know. Maybe we'll be old, settled-down, married guys at the same time."

"Yeah. I better go. Zoë's due home any minute."

"You guys are living together already?" The surprise was evident in Eli's voice.

"Well, not officially, but she's coming back to my place tonight for sure. We've also talked about letting you have her house while you're here. It's small, but it has everything you need, and it's way better than the local motel, especially now that the house has been fixed up."

Eli laughed, "For someone who's taken years to get there, you're certainly moving quickly now!"

Chuckling, Tanner answered, "Yeah. I can't let her think about anything and back out now."

"As if. Night, Tan. Kiss Zoë for me."

"Sure. Night, Eli."

"Wait," Eli commanded. Tanner didn't hang up. "I really am happy for you, man."

"Thanks, Eli." They disconnected simultaneously.

Chapter Sixteen

Christmastime was a sweet, happy occasion filled with local pageants and carolers. The Honeybee Hollow residents embraced the pageantry and the schmaltz of the season with zeal. Everyone tried to outdo each other by festooning their houses and yards with lights and gaudy decorations, and the entire town seemed to smell like pine boughs and mulled cider. Each of the businesses along Main Street had cookies or candy canes set out for shoppers, and Mayor Lassiter wore a red and green plaid vest under his suit jacket for most of December. The local kindergarten teacher often wore red tights and Christmas earrings, making her look like a beautiful Santa's helper.

On Christmas Eve, Zoë got a call from her parents who sounded a little high. They wished her a Happy Winter Solstice, even though they were actually off by a couple of days.

"Are you still in San Francisco?" she asked them.

Zoë's mom replied, "We're not too far from there. We found a place to work, so we're making some cash. You'd love the people we've met, Zoë. They're so well-informed and down to earth."

"This place has great benefits too," cackled her dad.

Grimacing a little, knowing that her parents tended to be overly influenced by blowhards and fools, Zoë answered, "That's great. I'm glad you're enjoying yourselves." After a little more conversation, Zoë discovered they were working on a pot farm. *At least it's legal now in California—not that they'd have cared much if it weren't. So, I guess 'the benefits' aren't in the form of a 401k—more like free samples.* "Merry Christmas to both of you." She was going to tell them about Tanner, but they hadn't asked her a single question about herself, and suddenly they were gone. Zoë *was* happy for them, though she still felt somewhat abandoned. She wondered what they'd make of her dating the mayor.

Tanner and Zoë went to the midnight Christmas service at the local Episcopal Church after her call. Tanner's parents were also MIA as they'd elected to take a seven-day Christmas cruise around the Caribbean. So, Christmas was a quiet day for them that they spent mostly in bed.

The day after Christmas, however, a messenger arrived and presented both of them with command performance invitations to a New Year's Eve party at Halden Dahl's house in Louisville. They were instructed to wear formal attire, and a limousine would be taking them to and from the party.

Zoë couldn't stand it, so she called her best friend, Madison, and put her on speakerphone and had Tanner sitting with her. "Merry Christmas, Madison! What's the deal with the fancy invitation?"

Tanner also chimed in, "Merry Christmas, Sis! Yeah, what gives? Your boyfriend sure seems to know how to get people's attention about a party."

They could hear Madison asking Halden to come join the conversation and said, "We're both here now, and you're on speaker too." Her voice sounded a little tired to Zoë, who chalked it up to too much Christmas cheer. But Madison went on, "Please don't tell anyone else who's invited, but we wanted you two to know that Halden and I are getting married that night, and we want you both to stand up for us. Zoë, will you be my maid of honor?"

Gasping with delight, Zoë gushed, "I'd love to. Ohmygod, this is wonderful!"

Breaking into the conversation, Halden said, "Tanner, will you be my groomsman? My brother Gunnar is my best man, and his wife Åse is great friends now with Madison, so she's going to also be a bridesmaid for her. We're keeping this whole thing as small as possible."

"Thanks, Halden. I'd be honored to be in the wedding party. Congratulations to both of you!"

Chapter Seventeen

Over the next couple of days, Tanner and Zoë took care of moving the rest of her things into his house. Finally, tired from lifting and carrying things, Tanner sat on the bed and took a look at a box full of paperback books that Zoë apparently hadn't been able to part with. As Zoë continued to hang her clothes in the closet, he smiled.

Several of them seemed to be by the same author—one he'd seen in his sister's possession from time to time—Dolly Gunn. Tanner pulled the top book off the stack and saw that it was well-worn and earmarked in quite a few places. The cover showed the naked torsos of two muscular men with a woman standing between them, and the title was *Two Times the Fun*. Snickering, he heard Zoë close the closet door, so he quickly slid the book back into the box.

Sitting down, Zoë snuggled up to him.

"So, read any good books lately?" he asked breezily.

"Actually, I have. How about you?" she asked without taking the bait.

"I haven't had much time for pleasure reading, I've mostly been working as much as possible on how to run for governor." Tanner was going to just make the minimum age requirement to become governor by a week, and he wanted the job passionately. To change the subject back to Zoë, however, he pointed out, "I see quite a few Dolly Gunn books on your shelf here. Doesn't Madison read those too?"

"Uh-huh," she said with a nod. "I introduced Madison to Dolly Gunn. You can always count on a romance author to put you in a good mood. I love that there are guaranteed happy endings. Life is so hard sometimes. It's great escapism."

"They look more like light porn to me with all the half-naked guys on the covers," he observed.

Zoë laughed, "Some people refer to this genre as Mommy Porn. And I don't deny the books are hot."

"Do you have a favorite?" he probed.

Zoë sat back. "Tanner, what's the deal with all the probing questions about my reading material? I like racy books. Is there something wrong with that?"

He laughed, "Nothing wrong in the least. I like the idea, but I never saw you as a threesome kind of woman."

Blinking at him she squeaked, "Me? What are you talking about?"

Tanner leaned forward and pulled out *Two Times the Fun* again and opened it to a page where the corner was folded down. He began to read at a random spot:

Isabelle could feel both cocks rubbing each other deep inside her. The feeling was like nothing she had ever imagined. Ramone lay behind her, grunting as he thrust into her over and over. The feeling was exquisite torture. Tristan impaled her from the front, and he moaned with his own pleasure, rhythmically grinding against her clit with his pubic bone. Her excitement grew with each pounding entry of her hard men. They crooned loving words into her ears as they writhed with ecstasy. Finally, all three of them cried out their release.

"Well!" Tanner cleared his throat, realizing he had a titanium boner now. "That's certainly something."

Zoë blushed and answered, "It's just a harmless fantasy."

***

Tanner had thought he'd propose on New Year's, but he didn't want to take the focus off of his sister's wedding. Still—he had a ring now that was perfect, and it was burning a hole in his pocket. When he saw Zoë, all decked out in a gorgeous off-the-shoulder formal gown with her long hair done in a becoming and complicated updo with sweet tendrils falling gracefully around her kissable face, he couldn't take it any longer. Just before the limo was due to arrive to take them along with his parents to Louisville, he stopped her in the living room and dropped to one knee. "Zoë, you are the woman of my dreams. I've loved you since I was seven years old—never stopped for one single day. Will you marry me and make me the luckiest and happiest man alive?"

Zoë blinked a few times, and her right hand went to her heart. "Tanner!" He produced a ring and clasped her left hand. As he slid it onto her finger, she smiled sweetly and answered, "Yes."

***

Madison and Halden's wedding was a small, formal affair at Halden's place with just their families and closest friends in attendance. It wasn't until after the beautiful, though brief, ceremony was over that Tanner and Zoë quietly let Madison and Halden know that they'd just gotten engaged. Madison was bursting with excitement, exclaiming, "Zoë, this is the happiest day of my life! Not only did I marry Halden, now my brother has his act together finally, and he's making you my *sister*. This is fantastic!" Then she hugged Zoë and Tanner, who looked over the moon.

***

On the limo ride home the next day, Tanner's mother, who was beside herself with happiness about their news, seemed to need to take over their wedding arrangements. She hadn't been consulted about her daughter's plans, and she apparently needed to plan someone's wedding—so why not her son's?

Zoë and Tanner were touched by this and knew to accept with grace. Tanner's campaign was ramping up, and that left him with no extra time at all, and Zoë had her hands full keeping up with school and Tanner.

The wedding was set to take place on Valentine's Day— that would fall on a Saturday that year. Mrs. Lassiter contacted her library guild and book club members, the ladies at the Episcopal Church, the school board, the town council, and any random friend she could think of to pitch in and help. The Sewing Bees—the Honeybee Hollow stitchery club—immediately invited Zoë to come to their meeting for a fitting and showed her dozens of dress ideas that they offered to make for her completely gratis. When Madison heard about this, she donated whatever materials they needed for the dress as she could get everything at a huge discount through her business. Zoë was so touched by everyone's thoughtfulness and generosity she could barely see the dress photos through her tears.

When the handsome and most beloved young mayor decides to marry the beautiful and equally beloved kindergarten teacher in a town like Honeybee Hollow, it not only makes the news, it becomes a civic event. Meetings were held all over town for the various committees, and everyone had a job to do that they did with joy.

Eli made sure the press stayed well-informed. He was in his element.

The town became even better known throughout Kentucky, and Tanner's name seemed to be on the tip of everyone's tongue. It was the sweetest love story ever, especially when the society bloggers got wind of the fact that the bride and groom had been friends virtually their whole lives. Someone dug up an old photo of the two of them at around six and seven years old, holding ice cream cones and watching the town's Fourth of July parade. Even then, Tanner hand his arm around Zoë and they were laughing. It was frequently juxtaposed next to their formal engagement photo and melted many a heart.

On February first, Eli was scheduled to arrive in town, and Tanner was thrilled that his best friend would be there. It was time for Eli to pitch in not only as best man, but also as Tanner's campaign manager. He needed to be hands-on from here on out rather than controlling things from a distance. He'd already hired a staff who had been working from campaign headquarters located in an office complex in town. The primaries would be in June, so there was a ton of work to do. He had Tanner booked into all sorts of speaking engagements all over the state, making it easy on him by using Eli's own private plane and pilot to get around the state and back home to Honeybee Hollow again.

Flying around the state wouldn't the most fuel-efficient way to go, but Tanner still had to do his job as mayor, so he planned to crisscross the state, wowing possible voters.

Chapter Eighteen

The day Eli arrived, Tanner and Zoë offered to meet him at the nearest municipal airport. However, Eli had also employed a limo company that would chauffeur Tanner and him all over with the added protection of security. So, on Sunday, February first, they waited anxiously for him to arrive. And finally, as a limo pulled up in front of the house, Tanner, who'd been looking eagerly out the front window, hurried to the door and rushed outside. Zoë was a bit slower, but right behind him.

The first thing Zoë noticed was that experiencing Eli's arrival was like watching the Oscars. The limo door opened, and out stepped the most incredibly beautiful man she'd ever imagined. Tall, lean, and broad-shouldered, tousled black hair, with penetrating eyes that went straight to Tanner's face. His bright smile was welcoming and genuine. She could almost imagine flashbulbs going off as the paparazzi recorded his entrance on the red carpet. *How could Tanner ever get anything done around so much physical beauty? Oh, that's dumb. He's a guy. Guys don't think that kind of thing about other men. And stop perving on Eli. Tanner's gorgeous too—and your fiancé!*

The next thing she noticed as she mentally fanned her face was their bro-hug. *They sure are happy to see each other!* She knew they were close, and they hadn't seen each other in a couple of months. If the hug went on a little too long, she failed to note that. Zoë also failed to register their undercurrent of melancholy and desperation, for at that moment, she noticed the final thing.

Mid-hug, Eli's eyes shifted to Zoë. When their eyes met, it was as if his hazel stare made a laser beam go straight through her. The expression on his face morphed from happiness to shock and a sense of recognition when he focused on her. It was only for a second, but it was there. Quickly, Eli schooled his features into a friendly smile as he broke loose from Tanner's embrace. He stalked toward Zoë with the confidence of a runway model and gently put his arms around her.

"Zoë, it's so good to finally meet you," he purred in her ear and then he kissed her cheek. "I feel as if I've known you for years—through Tanner, of course."

Zoë stood stock still, not knowing what to make of it as a frisson of desire streaked through her body with that one tiny, little, hardly-there peck on the cheek. She had to make a conscious effort to close her mouth because she knew she was gaping at him. Shaking herself mentally, she stepped back and offered her hand. "Eli, it's... um... so good to finally meet you too. Tanner says nothing but the nicest things about you always."

When Eli took her hand and enveloped it in his large, warm one, Zoë wondered, *Holy cow! What's wrong with me? I love Tanner!*

And just then, the man in question broke into Zoë's reverie and exclaimed, "God, it's so good to have my two favorite people in the whole world together with me finally. Come on in, Eli. We have lots to catch up on and lots to discuss." Tanner led them into his house. "We'll have lunch and then we'll get you settled over in Zoë's house. She's all moved in here with me now, so that place is free for you to use."

Zoë also explained, "It's small, but you ought to be comfortable enough. We had the furnace fixed finally, so that's not a problem anymore." She gave him a sweet smile that he returned.

Those hazel eyes of his bore into her once again as Eli said, "I'm sorry to put you out of your house, Zoë, but I'm sure that living with Tanner full-time is no hardship. I know he was always the best roommate I could have ever hoped for at college." He smiled at Tanner then and continued, "And you'll be married in two weeks anyway, so I guess this makes good sense." He looked back at Zoë and asked, "How are the wedding plans going?"

Laughing, Zoë began to relax. "The plans are going well. The entire town has turned our wedding into the event of the century and, spearheaded by Tanner's mother, there are committees upon committees taking care of every last detail. I think all Tanner and I have to do is show up at St. Mark's on time and say the right words."

"Honeybee Hollow certainly is a pretty town. When we drove in, I had this strong sense of Mayberry, USA," Eli laughed. "And now that I hear what the residents are doing for you, it seems like a wonderful place." He regarded Tanner carefully. "It's a little late to ask, but are you *sure* you're willing to give this up and move into the governor's mansion up in Frankfort?"

Tanner, who was sitting on the couch next to Zoë, took her hand and looked at Eli. "We're sure. Zoë knows she'll have to give up her classroom teaching job here, but we're both ready. A small town is great, but we have our sights set on something a lot bigger."

Zoë chimed in, "It's going to be bittersweet after the way the town has embraced us, but they also give us both constant encouragement to reach for the governorship. They know Tanner is destined for great things, and he's put the town on the map already. It's like we have this huge family behind us, cheering us along." She smiled brightly and felt herself relax even further. "I'll just go put lunch together. It'll just take a few minutes, and I'm sure y'all have some catching up to do."

As Zoë headed to the kitchen, she overheard Eli say, "Jesus, Tanner. You said she was something special, but I had no fucking idea!"

Tanner made a satisfied sounding chuckle. "Yeah."

Chapter Nineteen

The next two weeks were a whirlwind of last-minute wedding preparations and short-range trips for Tanner's campaign speeches. There was one strange thing going on, however, that Zoë didn't understand how to grasp.

Every so often, she would catch sight of Tanner and Eli interacting with one another. They were clearly close friends who shared a mutual affection, but there was an unmistakable air of melancholy between them. She couldn't put her finger on it, but at first it worried her that possibly Eli might be sick or something. She knew Tanner was alright. Then other times, she could swear their bodies wanted to gravitate to one another. The energy that flowed between the two men was palpable as she watched both of them resting their hands a few inches apart on the tabletop when they sat discussing some speech or strategy. It was as if they were touching without touching

Zoë didn't even know how to verbalize a question about her strange feeling, so she kept quiet. She did have her suspicions, however, that maybe there was more to their friendship than she'd thought. She decided to keep her eyes and ears open.

A few times over the next couple of weeks before the wedding, Zoë had the chance to spend time just with Eli. She found him as charming as he was attractive, and their conversations always felt like old friends rather than new acquaintances. She couldn't help feel a draw to him and noticed that Eli looked at her the same way he looked at Tanner on many occasions. She started watching him interact with others, but there was never the same electricity as when Eli was with one of them.

The sadness seemed to grow by the day, however, as they approached the wedding. Zoë was pretty sure by now that she knew the cause. Eli and Tanner were both suffering broken hearts. She loved Tanner so much, and she was becoming very fond of Eli, and their suffering was beginning to break her heart as well. She just didn't know how to broach the subject and figured it was their business.

***

And then finally, the wedding day was upon them. The church was booked for a 6:00 pm service, after which the reception would be held in the parish hall. Lucky for them, the Episcopal Church had a large hall because the crowd was going to be enormous. But even so, they finally decided to add to the square footage for the party-goers by erecting a large tent on the church grounds for the overflow. The parish hall had double doors that fed seamlessly right into the tent, and with lots of space heaters it would be perfect.

Despite all of the careful planning, however, something always happens. And what happened was that Zoë's parents decided to show up for the blessed nuptials of their beloved daughter. They'd never said a word to Zoë about whether or not they'd be there, so she'd just chalked their silence up to their general spaciness and self-importance. That, and she never *exactly* told them the date—she just mentioned to them that she'd be getting married to Tanner.

At 7:30 in the morning, Eli was rudely awakened by angry pounding on the kitchen door. He could hear a raised voice saying, "Hey, let us in, you ungrateful little brat!" And a deeper voice shouted, "This is still our house too, you know!"

Attired only in pajama bottoms, Eli squinted at a frowning couple as he opened the door. They were about the oddest people he'd ever encountered and, coming from New York, that was saying a lot. Dressed head to toe in tie-dye and leather with long, flyaway brown hair streaked with pink and blue, the woman gawked at his bare chest and then adopted a flirty tone. "Well, well! You're not Tanner. Who are you, you delicious young stud? And what are you doing in our house?" Her voice became a little shrill finally as she continued, "And why are we locked out?" She wore a cheesy green crown on her head that had a marijuana leaf motif and was emblazoned with the word "Highness" across the front. The crown wobbled as she berated him.

The man, whose salt and pepper hair was nearly as long as his wife's and who sported a scraggly beard that stretched halfway to the waistline of his filthy jeans, grumbled, "It's cold as fuck out here, Junior! Let us in!" Apparently, his fringed buckskin jacket was no match for the weather. Both of them wore sandals that were completely inappropriate for February, and their toes were turning blue.

With every ounce of courtesy he could muster, Eli stepped backward into the cramped kitchen and explained, "Mr. and Mrs. Deliban. I'm Elison Whittaker, Tanner's best man. I'm sure they didn't know you'd be arriving, or they'd have made other housing arrangements for me. My apologies."

"Are you sleepin' here with my daughter?" demanded Mr. Deliban. "If so, I'm glad to see she's not limiting herself to just the mayor. A young woman needs to explore her options."

"Sir, please. Why don't you both have a seat, and I'll make us some coffee. Zoë isn't here. She's over at Tanner's house." He waited for them to plunk themselves down at the kitchen table and flipped the coffee maker on, saying, "If you'll excuse me, I'll be right back. It's a little chilly in here, and I'd like to get more clothes on."

"Not on my account!" giggled Mrs. Deliban.

Eli made a beeline for the bedroom and dressed as quickly as possible in jeans and a heavy sweater. He sat to tie his shoes when he became aware of a distinctive aroma wafting through the house that was *not* coffee and toast. The aging hippies had decided to light up in the kitchen. "Oh great," Eli muttered. *This is going to be a hell of a day with these two around. I need to talk to Tanner right away.*

Heading back into the kitchen, Eli saw that the room was already smoke-filled. He wanted to crack open a window, but it was freakishly cold, even for February. Thinking fast, Eli stepped back out of the room and Googled something quickly with his phone, shook his head with a grimace, and then called his driver to come pick him up as quickly as possible. Fortunately, Eli had not unpacked most of his clothes yet, and his tux was still in his travel bag.

Re-entering the kitchen, Eli announced, "Help yourself to the coffee. I think Zoë stocked the refrigerator with plenty of food for me... I mean for you. I'll be getting out of your way now. I'm sorry for the disturbance. I'll just go find somewhere else to stay."

"Zoë's always been kind of a scatterbrain," her father chuckled and gave a dismissive wave of his heavily tattooed hand. "No harm done, Junior. We'll see ya at the weddin'." He frowned then and grumbled, "It was damn rude to find out from the internet that the weddin' was today instead of from our ungrateful daughter."

Eli was quite sure Zoë was not a scatterbrain, and he had no idea why she'd be considered ungrateful for anything, but he didn't want to get into it with this weirdo. The man seemed to run hot and cold at the drop of a hat. Then, Eli stepped backward as Mrs. Deliban thrust a bony hand towards him with an enormous joint in it. "Care for a hit, cutie pie?" she giggled.

"It'll loosen that stick you have up your ass. This is the good stuff we helped grow out in Cali!"

"No thank you, Mrs. Deliban. And you both know, don't you, that marijuana is still illegal in Kentucky unless it's taken orally for medicinal purposes under strict guidelines?"

"Pfft!" she exclaimed. "Stupid hillbillies." Leering at him, she offered, "If you can't find anywhere else to stay, you can always come back here and sleep with me. I can teach you a thing or two." She licked her lips, and then giggled.

Eli's eyebrows shot up into his hairline, and he was relieved to feel his phone buzz with a text telling him that the driver was here. "Well, in any case, I'll see you both later." Eli and his baggage were out of there and into the limo in record time.

He quickly told the driver, "Take me to Tanner's house please." He figured he'd better send his buddy a text and let him know he was on his way at least. No sense in another rude awakening this morning.

Eli: Hey Tan. There's trouble in Mayberry. I've been kicked out and I'm on my way over now.

Within seconds, Eli got Tanner's reply:

Tanner: WTF??

Eli: The hippies are in town. Mrs. D wants to jump my bones and they have drugs. Pot for sure- maybe more.

Tanner: Well shit.

Less than ten minutes later, Eli stood on Tanner's front porch looking distraught and smelling like a doob. Tanner opened the door and gave a little cough. "Come on in. Any great idea on what we're going to do about them?"

"What *can* we do? They're Zoë's family," Eli pointed out frantically. "I just didn't quite get the message about what weirdos they were. We're going to somehow keep them away—*far away*—from any of the press who're likely to show up tonight. This could be a disaster!"

Just then, Zoë entered the room, and Eli was struck once more by her unbelievable beauty and his inappropriate desire for her. He sucked in a breath thinking that this wedding was going to kill him in one way or another. The mother and father of the bride had the potential of completely ruining the groundwork he'd carefully laid out for Tanner's path to the governor's mansion, and now *he* had a major case of the hots for the bride. This was an unmitigated mess. He needed to regain control over the situation immediately.

Tanner broke into Eli's inner turmoil, asking, "Do you want to stay here?"

"What?" Eli's voice cracked. "Why? Isn't there a motel nearby?"

Tanner smiled and explained, "There's a motel, but it's been full for weeks. You know that. You've brought in campaign specialists, and we have out-of-town wedding guests there too. Everyone is doubling up and filling every last room. So, your choices are to go back and stay in Zoë's house with the parents or stay here in the guest room. Zoë stayed in it last night so we wouldn't sleep together the night before the wedding, but she sure isn't going to be in there tonight." He gave Eli a wink. "I'm also sorry to say my parents' house is full of family, so there's no room there either."

There was no time for a honeymoon with the school year still going on and the campaign in full swing, so they'd planned to take one later when they could enjoy a little respite. Eli could just imagine what it would be like staying here under those conditions.

Looking helplessly at Zoë, Eli asked, "Uh... if you didn't want to sleep with Tanner, why are you here now? Aren't you supposed to not see each other before the wedding?"

Zoë shrugged her shoulders and smiled. "We decided that was a dumb tradition, but the not sleeping together would just make tonight more exciting." She had the courtesy to blush. "So, now that you've met my parents, and you understand the trouble they might cause, do you want me to do something about them?"

Furrowing his brow, Eli asked, "Zoë, do you want them at the wedding? This is really up to you. Say the word, and I'll make sure they stay away, but if you want them there, we need to do some serious damage control."

Zoë thought for a moment and answered cautiously, "I know they're kooks, but they're the only parents I have. So, yes, I would like them there. I'm happy they cared enough finally to show up actually. I didn't give them a lot of details because, frankly, I was scared to be disappointed again if they flaked out on me." She looked at Tanner. "On the other hand, I know how important your career is to you, and I don't want to be the source for any embarrassment."

Tanner immediately swept Zoë into his arms and assured her, "Nothing about you could ever be less than perfect in my eyes. We'll just have to deal with them the best we can." He looked imploringly at Eli for guidance.

"Alright. Let me just go bring my stuff in from the car and the I'll make some calls. I have a few ideas." Eli looked at Zoë, asking, "Do you have another key to the house? I need to go back and give one to your parents. They're in it now, but if they leave, they could end up locked out."

"Sure, Eli, but why do you need the extra one?" she asked quizzically.

"More damage control."

Chapter Twenty

A couple of hours later, Eli showed up again at Zoë's house offering the key to Mrs. Deliban with the explanation, "I'm sorry I forgot to give this to you earlier." He hid a grimace as she stroked his hand while accepting the key with a suggestive grin. Ignoring her look, he continued, "As a courtesy to both of you—being VIP guests and all—some stylists are going to be here in an hour or so. They'll make sure you have the full spa treatment and complimentary wardrobe for tonight. Please comply with everything they tell you to wear and do."

Mr. Deliban appeared behind his wife asking, "Why should we, Junior? Ain't we good enough for you?"

Plastering on what he hoped looked like a congenial smile, Eli explained, "Mr. and Mrs. Deliban, I'm sure you're aware that Tanner is a prominent political leader in this town and he is currently running for governor. Wouldn't you love to see your daughter as first lady of Kentucky?" He felt bolstered as he saw the couple both stand a little taller and watched as their eyes grew brighter, so he forged ahead with his next plan. "And if you comply with the stylists, I'll pay you ten thousand dollars. Cash."

"Well! Now yer talkin', Junior!" Mr. Deliban crowed. "Bring 'em on. We can be as hoity-toity as *you* for that kind of persuasion."

Eli gave a mental fist pump and patted his own back. *I knew it! The greedy creep.* "Just one more thing. If a member of the press should ask you anything, just smile politely and tell them you don't wish to be bothered on your daughter's special day. Can you do that?" Eli reached into his pocket and produced an enormous wad of hundred-dollar bills. "Here's half now and I'll give you the other half later. If you behave." He watched as they stared at the cash with greedy expressions. They both nodded agreeably, so he handed over the money. "Ah, I hear a car pulling up now, so I think the wardrobe stylists are here already. I'll leave you to them. Later a driver will take you to the local salon for haircuts for both of you and makeup for Mrs. Deliban."

***

Later that afternoon, as soon as the driver left with the Delibans for their appointments, a man arrived at the house accompanied by a German Shepherd. He let himself into the house with a key, telling the dog, "Okay, Fritz, let's get to work, good boy!" Less than twenty minutes later, they left the house, this time with a large, very full bag. They then proceeded to check out the interior of the van that was parked in the driveway, and added a few more items to the bag. With a satisfied smile and a big treat for the dog, he drove off.

***

When the Delibans arrived at the church that evening, they marched up to Eli and Mr. Deliban announced in a stage whisper, "We were robbed while we were out of the house, Junior! You wouldn't happen to know anythin' about that, now would ya?"

With a serene look, Eli assured him, "You were not robbed. Everything has been relocated to a safe place for you, and if you manage to not make a scene, as soon as you leave to go back to California, it will all be returned."

"Humph. You had no right," he grumbled.

"I wanted to make sure no one landed *in jail.* Now remember, act polite tonight and stay away from reporters or you won't see the other five grand *or* your stash," Eli promised. "Now, Mr. Deliban, your daughter awaits you in the anteroom to the right of the main entrance. And, Mrs. Deliban, as soon as we hang up your coat, it would be my honor to escort you to your seat. You look lovely, I might add."

Mr. Deliban grumbled and wandered away, and Mrs. Deliban simpered at him. When she returned to Eli's side in the church's vestibule, he noticed that she really did look pretty in her understated blue chiffon gown. She had Zoë's lovely brown eyes, and as long as she didn't say anything, he could appreciate her attractiveness. She ruined the whole thing however, when, as he offered her his arm, she reached around and pinched his butt, exclaiming, "Ooh! Nice and tight. You must work out a lot."

Eli glared at her a second, then morphed his features back into polite nonchalance. He stuffed her hand into the crook of his arm and asked, "Shall we?" They made their way up the aisle at a sedate pace, and Eli sent up a silent prayer to the Jesus behind the altar that this crazy woman and her husband would behave themselves. She nodded and grinned and blew air kisses at people all the way through the church as though she were the proud hostess, even though she hadn't done so much as lift a finger in preparation for this day. The Delibans were a couple of loose cannons. Eli thought this day could not be over soon enough.

Not too long after that, Eli and Tanner took their places up in front along with the other groomsmen—two old buddies of Tanner's from way back, his brother-in-law Halden, and a guy from the town council. Eli eyed Tanner to see if he could detect any nerves or reservation, but all he saw was a man in love who was eager for the ceremony to be over.

The music changed. Zoë and her father approached the altar where Tanner and all of the attendants stood. Eli finally appreciated how transformed Mr. Deliban looked. His ratty beard was trimmed stylishly, and his crazy head of hair was considerably shorter and slicked back into a somewhat respectable ponytail at the nape of his neck. *It's the best I could have hoped for, I guess. Maybe people will just think the old guy looks artistic.*

Then Eli looked at Zoë and wished he hadn't. She was the most stunningly perfect woman he ever clapped eyes on and seemed to glow in her elegant gown and veil. Her eyes were glued to Tanner as she and her father made their way forward. Eli felt himself, much to his mortification, growing hard just looking at her. *Thank God for my jacket.* But then, it got worse. Zoë's eyes flicked over to Eli for a moment, and he saw what looked like desire in them directed his way too. *Oh shit!* It was over in a flash, but he'd registered it. Zoë had looked at him with that same sense of recognition he'd seen in her before, and then after a split second of confusion, she dragged her eyes back to Tanner. Eli hoped to hell Tanner hadn't noticed that look.

The ceremony was pure torture for Eli. He stood next to the man he loved and watched him pledge his life to the woman Eli lusted for and had no right to think of in such a way. He burned with jealousy for both of them. His hands shook when he handed Tanner the ring, and he tried to ignore the familiar feel of Tanner's hand on his.

Somehow, he made it through the wedding and the reception and even managed a coherent speech about how proud he was of his best friend and how happy he was for the couple. *Yeah, sure.* Mostly his heart just bled a little each time the couple kissed each other.

Eli drank a lot of champagne, and then switched over to bourbon. He danced and tried to chat up people, reminding them all in subtle ways to get out and vote for Tanner in the June primaries. Finally, completely drained emotionally, he went to sit with his parents and his sister who'd flown in from New York for the wedding. After a while, his parents drifted off to socialize, leaving the siblings at the table. His sister Caro kept narrowing her eyes at Eli as if she wondered what was going on in his head.

"Eli," she started gently, "would you like some more help with Tanner's campaign?" He raised his head and looked at her quizzically. "I have some time for the next few months that I could take off and come back down here and lend you a hand. I'm sure you have things under control, but—many hands make light labor, or however the saying goes. I'm here to help, if you'd like."

Eli considered her offer. Caro had matured into a level-headed young woman now that her rock 'n' roll days were behind her, and she was great with people. Smiling at her fondly, he answered, "Sure, Caro. Thank you. I'd love to have you here. I know Tanner would gladly have the extra support, and you'll love getting to know Zoë." He lowered his voice to a conspiratorial level, saying, "Once we get her nutty parents out of town, there will be room in the house for you to stay with me. Just let me know when you can be here. Hopefully they'll be out of our hair soon."

Caro looked perplexed. "Don't they want to stay here in their own house?"

Eli chuckled, "It's actually debatable apparently whether it's theirs. They abandoned it to Zoë years ago so she'd be pretty much forced to continue paying the taxes on it as well as the mortgage they'd taken out on it. They said verbally that it was hers, but I guess no one ever bothered to get that in writing.

In any case, I think I can persuade them to head back to California to continue their 'careers' there." Caro looked questioningly at him, but he shook his head. "A topic for a private conversation another day."

At that point, their parents returned to the table. They'd been chatting like old friends with Tanner's parents. Eli's dad announced, "Son, we had a great time tonight and it's good to see you. I hope you can get our boy into the governor's mansion without a hitch. It goes without saying, let me know if I can do anything at all to help. Now, Caro, we need to head back. Let's get going, shall we?"

This left Eli alone with his wretched thoughts. He wished he could say he'd had a wonderful time tonight. Scanning the crowd for someone to talk to, he gave up and nursed another glass of bourbon—in a complete shit mood. He knew in his heart that the ceremony was moving and the reception was wonderful in a small-town kind of way that ought to have warmed his heart, but his heart was too broken to feel any of it.

They took separate limos back to Tanner's house—now Tanner and Zoë's, he corrected himself. Eli tried to give them as much privacy as possible, so he waited another miserable half an hour before taking off. He desperately wanted to go to sleep and forget this thoroughly exhausting episode.

Eli had lied to Tanner for the past several years. He'd made it sound as if he'd been out on dates quite often and was looking for a suitable wife and just hadn't found her yet. But the truth was, he'd only been on a few dates that were basically forced on him by his parents. He lived for the fishing trips he and Tanner took every couple of months. After telling Tanner over and over to marry Zoë, he tried to make himself believe that was the best thing for Tanner and his political goals, but it was killing him inside. And now, it was done. Eli had no idea how to handle this new reality.

The house was dark when he returned, so he made his way quietly to his bedroom. He yanked off his tux and pulled on his flannel pajama pants. After brushing the taste of wedding cake and bourbon out of his mouth, he flopped onto his bed. And then the worst happened. The sounds of lovemaking from down the hall penetrated his consciousness. He knew those sounds all too well. He'd evoked them from Tanner himself for years. This time, however, Tanner's moans and words of endearment were accompanied by the sweetest sounds from Zoë. The noises grew louder and louder, and Eli tried to put a pillow over his ears to drown them out. His imagination filled in what he couldn't quite hear, however, torturing him even further. When the noises stopped, he thought maybe he could sleep, but that didn't happen. So, Eli thought maybe he needed one more drink. He crept out of his room and down the dark hall to figure out where Tanner kept his liquor. Unfortunately, he wasn't all that familiar with the layout of the house quite yet and crashed his bare foot into the leg of a table.

"Ow! Fuck!" he yelped and then tried to make himself shut up. He flopped down onto the couch with pain shooting through his foot and slumped his head down into his hands. It was then the tears started. He'd kept it together for as long as possible, but the dam broke finally. He sobbed quietly into his hands for a moment and then jumped when he felt someone sit down on the couch next to him. He didn't even have to look up to realize it was Tanner's strong, warm arms that wrapped around him and pulled him to his bare chest. He felt Tanner kiss the top of his head.

"I'm sorry, Eli. I'm so wrapped up in myself, I forgot how hard this has to be for you." Tanner stroked Eli's bare back and leaned his head over the top of Eli's. They sat there for a long time like that, skin to skin, stroking and holding each other. Neither of them heard the footsteps that approached, stopped for a while, and then retreated.

Chapter Twenty-One

When Zoë woke up after her latest and greatest orgasm of the night had exhausted her, she realized she'd heard an odd noise. Tanner wasn't in bed with her, and that confused her. Then she became curious when she realized she could hear Tanner's voice coming from the living room. Straining her ears, she couldn't hear what he was saying, but the tone was evident—soft and crooning, the way he sometimes sounded when they made love. *What on earth?*

Grabbing her robe, she tossed it on and made her way toward the front of the house.

The sight that greeted her in the moonlight peeking around the edges of the drapes on the front window took her breath away. Her new, beloved husband was embracing and stroking the back of his best man and campaign manager. They were both half-naked, and Eli seemed to be hiccupping in the aftermath of a good cry. She wondered what bothered Eli so terribly, but that thought was banished when she watched Tanner kiss the top of Eli's head and lean into him so that they were pressed together. This was clearly not a bro hug moment. Zoë didn't need any more confirmation than that.

Silently, she spun away and returned to bed.

But she couldn't force herself to get back into the bed she and Tanner had just messed up so deliciously with their lovemaking. Zoë paced and paced around the room, trying to make sense of what she'd seen and her reaction to it. Her head was a jumble.

At least twenty minutes crawled by, and Zoë was getting pissed off. How dare Tanner leave their bed on their wedding night to... do what? Snuggle up to Eli for a while? Burning with a temper by now, she stomped back down the hall and found the two men sound asleep. Tanner was lying on the couch with Eli draped over him, and they were still holding each other tightly.

Her body went rigid with emotion, and she clenched her fists, shrieking, "What the hell is going on?"

Jumping up like the fire alarm had just gone off in their station, both men jerked to their feet and looked at each other and then at Zoë. In the early morning light, she may as well have had steam pouring off of her for the rage she projected.

"Oh fuck," mumbled Eli, bringing his hand to his face and covering his eyes.

"I'm sorry!" cried Tanner, looking back and forth between Eli and Zoë, so it wasn't even evident whom he was addressing.

Zoë sunk down in an armchair across from them and looked like the wind had all just escaped from her sails. In a sad, choking whisper, she asked Tanner, "Am I just your *beard?* Or was it *that* important to you to have a wife for your stupid campaign that you had to trick me?"

"God, Zoë, no!" he cried. "Neither of those things."

Eli gave Tanner a look and asked, "Really?"

"Well, it was your idea, Eli. You've been saying for years I needed to marry Zoë and have some kids so I'd look stable and... white bread enough for the voters."

Zoë gasped and stood with a sob. She started to make her way back to the bedroom as she announced, "I'm packing my bags and going back to my own house. Eli, I need one of those keys—now."

Tanner zoomed around and stood in front of Zoë so she couldn't retreat any further down the hall. He reached for her, but she scooted back, colliding with Eli's naked chest, feeling his arms go around her as if by instinct. She gasped and turned in his arms, not knowing whether to be turned on by him in his semi-naked deliciousness or hate his miserable guts for ruining her life. She shook loose of him and stood panting in the hallway between the two men with tears running down her face.

"Why did you lie to me, Tanner?" She was near hysterics at this point. "Why did you *make me love you* and keep it from me that you were secretly gay all this time?" She roughly wiped her tears off with the back of her hand and whirled toward Eli. "And why do *you* keep looking at me like you want to eat me for lunch, Eli, if you're really in love with my husband? This is so fucked up!"

At the same time Eli backed up with a shocked expression, Tanner declared, "I never *made* you love me, Zoë. You've always loved me the same way I've always loved you—ever since we were kids, I've known we belonged together. And you knew it too. It just took us a long time to get here. That, and I majorly fucked up with you when I left for college." He gently stepped forward and led her back to the couch where he sat down with her, much the same way he'd done With Eli earlier. Eli sat on her other side several inches away.

Tanner crooned softly to her, "I love you, Zoë. So much. And I was going to tell you everything about Eli eventually, but since things are over between us, there was no rush."

Zoë interrupted, "Over? Things didn't look so *over* to me when I saw you kiss him and then found you both aslcep together likc... lovers!"

Grimacing, Tanner explained, "Yeah, I guess we were both pretty exhausted and just kind of fell asleep. That wasn't supposed to happen. But I have to be honest..."

"About time, don't you think?" she snapped at him.

"You're right. So, here goes." Tanner tried to take Zoë's hand but she crossed her arms and her legs like she wanted to be as small as possible. "I have never for one minute stopped loving you, Zoë. You have to believe that." She snorted, but he forged ahead. "And then I got to Princeton and met Eli." He looked beyond Zoë to his best friend who was looking at Zoë rather than at him. "I love Eli too. Like... the way I love you. I know it's confusing. I'm bisexual—but I've never even been attracted to *anyone* other than the two of you. Ever!"

Turning furious eyes on Tanner, Zoë hissed, "So you were... what? Going to keep poor Eli as your dirty little secret to screw on the side? You're even worse than Brandon!" She broke down into sobs so awful, Eli scooted over to her and wrapped his arm around her. For some reason she couldn't explain to herself, she let him.

"No, Zoë. It's not like that at all," Eli said in a voice that cracked with sorrow. "Believe him. Tanner promised years ago that we'd be finished if you'd ever take him back. He said he could never cheat on you. We haven't been together as lovers since you and he started your relationship again." Zoë wiped her nose on her sleeve and looked at him as he continued, "I still love him as much as I ever did, but we've been clear that marrying you was important. I encouraged him to marry you— that's true. He needs a wife if he's to be governor, but if I'm blunt... this decision is killing me."

Zoë looked confusedly at Tanner. "Bisexual?"

Tanner nodded. "I didn't even know it until I met Eli. I'd never felt that way when you and I were together... before college."

Zoë looked at Eli. "What about you?"

"Same... well, not really. I've actually known I was bi since I was about thirteen. It's not easy being in the middle ground because someone usually thinks you're faking or lying about your sexuality. I've had lovers of both sexes, but once I met Tanner that stopped, and it's only been Tanner since we were freshmen."

Zoë gasped. "It's been years, Eli!" He nodded and looked down. She squinted at him and asked, "Why do you keep looking at me like a starving man confronted with a cherry pie?"

Tanner sucked in a breath. "He does?"

Eli asked, "I do?"

"Oh come on, Eli. I've seen your expressions, and I'm not dumb," she stated firmly. "Are you attracted to me too? Is there another level of fucked-uppedness going on here?"

"Um," Eli hedged and then blurted out, "yes." He looked quickly to Tanner, saying, "As soon as I laid eyes on her, Tan, I realized just what you saw in Zoë. She's one in a million—no, a billion. I'm sorry to admit, even though I love you with all my heart, I saw her and suddenly had this overwhelming urge to... I don't know... throw her over my shoulder and run away with her or something."

Zoë put her head down into her hands, covering her face. "Oh, God," she muttered. "Thanks for the compliment, at least."

In a defeated voice, Eli continued, "I don't even know who to be more jealous of, frankly. So," he sighed, "I think I ought to just go back to New York and leave you both in peace. I promise I'll find you a good campaign manager to take my place, Tan." A tear leaked from the corner of his eye that he whisked away quickly.

"No one can take your place, Eli," Tanner moaned in a broken voice. "Maybe I should just be happy being mayor of Mayberry and forget my lofty aspirations." His attempt at humor brought a sad smile to Eli's face.

Zoë stood abruptly and announced, "I'm going to go make us all some coffee. Let's not make any rash decisions just yet. I... uh... I need to... think."

They both stared at her retreating back, not knowing what to say.

Chapter Twenty-Two

Zoë had needed to get away from them to clear her head. She could tell that Tanner and Eli were dying inside knowing they'd have to give each other up, and the obvious depth of their sadness broke her heart. She filled the coffee maker and stared at it unseeing as the machine did its job. Instead, she saw in her mind's eye the longing on their faces and knew Tanner had been faithful to her since Eli had come to town. The episode she'd witnessed had been innocent—just the two of them comforting each other.

Several minutes later, she returned with a tray of coffee and bagels that she set on the coffee table. They all reached for a cup, but the food sat untouched.

No one said a word. They all gripped their warm mugs like lifelines. The only promising part of the scenario was that Zoë voluntarily sat between them again instead of across the room in the armchair.

Finally, she broke the silence in a small, tentative voice. "Okay, you guys. Since it's time for brutal honesty all around, I guess it's my turn." Once she understood Tanner hadn't been using her as his beard, she'd considered the choices they had.

They both stared at her like they had no idea what would pop out of her mouth next. Tanner's eyes were full of worry, and Eli looked hopeful, as though he'd grab onto anything at this point.

First, she turned to Tanner and took a sip of coffee and then a deep breath. "I love you."

Tanner let out a long, relieved breath and gave her a warm smile. "That's so good to hear," he whispered as he reached to tuck a strand of hair behind her ear.

"But," she went on and his face fell momentarily, "I'm frankly not all that surprised about you and Eli. I know you so well, Tanner, and as much as I think you've been trying to hide your feelings for him, I've seen them. I just didn't understand." Eli let out a shocked gasp, and she turned his way. "In a glance at Eli, in your tone of voice when you speak about him and to him. It's all been there all along." She turned back to her husband. "You just have to be able to read the signs."

"I'm sorry, Zoë," Tanner began, but she put up a hand to gently silence him.

"No apologies. The heart wants what the heart wants. You love him, and you're lucky enough that Eli loves you back."

Tanner's mouth dropped open, and his eyes bugged a little. "You're not going to leave me now are you, Zoë?"

Softly, Zoë continued. "Hang on a sec, Tanner." She turned and said, "Eli, I'm flattered to pieces that you're so attracted to me, knowing the depth of your love for Tanner. He's easy to love, isn't he?" Eli smiled at her and nodded. "So, I have to confess to both of you, that I'm as attracted to Eli as he is to me."

With that, Eli jumped to his feet, exclaiming, "I *knew* it! Ow!" Then he blushed and sat back down quickly, grabbed a napkin and wiped away the coffee he'd sloshed on his bare chest. "Sorry. That was uncalled for. I don't mean to be a smug egotist."

For the first time that morning, Tanner and Zoë both laughed. Then she dropped one more bomb. "I came down the hall twice in the middle of the night, and the first time I saw you, you know what my reaction was?"

"Your husband is a rotten cheater?" asked Tanner with a grimace.

"Not even close." They both gaped at her as she explained, "I was shocked, but I thought to myself, 'they're so beautiful together.' I don't know, guys, but the sight of you kissing Eli, Tanner, and you two holding each other was incredibly moving and... um... it... well, it turned me on. It was only after I thought about it later that I got mad. I thought I'd been taken for a fool. I decided I must just be your beard. But now I can see that really isn't the case since you're *both* willing to give up your ambitions." She waited for a beat for that to sink in. "Yes, you should have told me sooner, and that does piss me off, but... well..." They waited nervously for her to finish her thought. "If two of us stay together as a couple—no matter which two— one of us will be shattered. So perhaps we can be like a tripod. They're built with three legs to be as strong and stable as possible. Maybe we can work with this. As a... oh, God, I can't even believe I'm thinking this... as a *threesome*. There. I said it. I'm *so* embarrassed now, you have no idea!"

The silence was deafening.

Eli looked at Tanner over Zoë's bent head. "Tan, do you think you could actually share Zoë? That's what she's asking."

Zoë answered before Tanner could reply. "Eli, can you say *you'd* share Tanner with me?" She turned to Tanner. "And Tanner, can you share Eli with me? I don't want to diminish anything the two of you have. You've obviously loved each other deeply for years. I can't be the reason you have to be torn apart."

"For once in my life," Tanner began, "I'm speechless." He looked into the brown eyes and then hazel eyes he loved so dearly and realized there was only one solution. Backing away from either of them would mean pain he'd have to deal with forever, and he already had a good idea of what that would feel like. On the other hand, trying to do something few people could accomplish successfully—and manage it secretly while living in the public eye—would be an enormous challenge. He looked into their expectant, hopeful faces and answered finally, "I think Zoë's right. We owe it to ourselves to try. I know for myself I'd always regret it if I tried to give up on either of you. I'm so happy with you, Zoë, but I can't deny something important is missing without Eli." He gave them both a smile. "What do you think, Eli? I'm sure Zoë means for you to be an equal partner in this scenario and not some side fun for us."

Zoë looked serious and confirmed, "That's exactly what I mean. I recognize that I don't know you as well, Eli, and it's going to take us some time to catch up to what we both have with Tanner, but I'm willing to make the effort to see if we can get there."

"How would this work?" asked Eli. "You know if this is to happen, we'd have to be even more careful now. This would rile up tons of people if they thought their governor-to-be was in a polyamorous relationship. We're not exactly on the liberal west coast here, you know?"

"We can be careful; we've had years of practice," Tanner stated. "Not everyone is as tuned into us as Zoë is. People will be oblivious as usual."

Eli was quiet as he looked at them and then reached for Zoë. "I think what you're proposing is a beautiful gift. I'm floored by you, Zoë." She relaxed into his embrace as Eli looked questioningly once more at Tanner. When Tanner smiled at him, Eli first kissed Zoë's forehead, then her cheek. He felt her body lean into him, so he kissed her sweetly on the lips. When she opened her mouth for him, he increased his pressure and explored her with his tongue.

"You're beautiful together too," Tanner declared softly. "Now I see just what Zoë saw when she found us together, Eli. It may be wrong to some people, but to me, it's so perfect. And," he gained volume with a smile, "If I'm blunt about it, you two together turn me on!"

Breaking the kiss and leaning back into Tanner's arms, Zoë laughed, "This has been one crazy wedding night, but how many women can say theirs ended up with two grooms instead of one? Lucky me?"

Eli leaned over and kissed her cheek. He whispered into her neck as he nuzzled her, "Lucky all of us. For myself, I thought I'd be losing Tanner for good, but instead I'm gaining two perfect lovers."

Tanner began to laugh. "I get to be Tristan, but Eli has to be *Ramone*," he said in a comical voice that made Zoë giggle.

Eli pulled back looking confused. "Who?"

"Our proper little schoolmarm here has a penchant for reading racy literature, and they're characters in one of her favorite MMF books." He wiggled his eyebrows as Zoë blushed.

"Cool," said Eli with a thoughtful nod and then frowned. "What's MMF?"

"It's what we are," explained Zoë. "Two bi guys and a woman. As opposed to MFM, which is kind of ridiculous. It sounds lots more plausible—and fun—if everyone is equally interested in all parties."

Looking thoughtful, Eli mused, "Ohh... I get it." Then he gave a little snort. "Maybe you can give us some pointers from your *research* then, Zoë."

Zoë looked at Tanner, then she looked at Eli. She turned and kissed Tanner, wrapping her arms around him tightly. After a long, passionate smooch, she broke off and turned to Eli. He winked at her, so she put her arms around him and leaned in for a kiss from him as well. Tanner leaned in and scooped Zoë's hair to the side so he could kiss her neck. She gave a tiny moan of pleasure, so he pulled the collar of her robe down and kissed down her neck and shoulder. All this time, she was lip-locked with Eli.

Finally, Zoë pulled away from Eli and looked him in the eye. "Kiss Tanner, Eli. I want to watch. She leaned back into the couch so the men could access each other right in front of her. They immediately grabbed for each other and crashed their mouths together. There was no finesse, just raw desire. "Oh, God, you guys. Oh, wow," she moaned. "I like this. A lot." Squeezing her legs together, she reached her hands up and dragged her fingers through both their hair and down their backs. She was outrageously turned on—and barely anything had happened.

Breaking their long kiss, Tanner looked at Zoë questioningly. He slowly opened the front of her robe so that her breasts were exposed. Simultaneously, both men leaned in to play with her nipples with their mouths. Tanner tended to open his mouth and take in a lot of Zoë's breast, and Eli was a nibbler. He licked and played with her with his mouth, and then bit down sharply on her sensitive nipple. Zoë gave a surprised gasp and then a purr. She gently pushed them both away. "I know it's still barely the crack of dawn, guys, but just in case someone comes to the door, why don't we take this to the bedroom?"

Eli started to laugh, and she looked questioningly at him. He explained, "I take it you didn't see that someone hung a Do Not Disturb sign on your front door?'

Tanner grinned and said, "It's going to be a very short honeymoon, and I didn't want to be bothered. You know how the people are in this town. Someone is always bound to stop by with a pie or a casserole." He rose from the couch, extending a hand to both of his lovers, leading them down the hall to the master bedroom.

Eli followed them chuckling, "Mayor Lassiter arrested for petty crime. Caught swiping a room sign from the Skylark Motel. Film at eleven."

"Hey, we needed it more than they did!"

Zoë rolled her eyes. "Don't get any ideas about flipping the sign over if the house gets messy."

Entering the bedroom, they all three stared at the rumpled bed. It's one thing to say you're going to suddenly be a threesome, but the logistics of it are tricky. One would begin to say something and stop, then another. Finally, Zoë asked, "Why don't you guys get naked?" Instantly two pairs of flannel pants hit the floor, and it was as clear as day they were both aroused. "Now show me something," she ordered.

They looked at her questioningly, so she explained, "I want to see you make love to each other."

Eli fairly trembled with his excitement and looked longingly at Tanner's erection. There was no disguising his craving.

In a soft, seductive voice, Zoë crooned, "Do it, Eli. Whatever it is you want. Do it for Tanner and show me."

Eli's knees hit the floor, and he hungrily engulfed Tanner's engorged dick into his mouth. Tanner let out a hiss of pleasure, and reached for Zoë. He pulled her to his side and held her closely. "This is amazing," he whispered.

Zoë's face turned pink as she watched. This was the hottest thing she'd ever imagined being part of, and she could feel her own wetness dampening her bare thighs. Tanner bent his head and began to suck on her breast as he groaned his own pleasure at Eli's ministrations. He stopped for a moment then and slowly slid her robe off to the floor.

Eli sat back, grabbing his hand around Tanner and continuing to stroke him as he watched Tanner playing with Zoë's nipple. He clearly enjoyed his first sight of Zoë naked. Still watching the two of them, Eli put his mouth back on Tanner and continued to suck on him with long, hard pulls.

Zoë gave a tiny flinch of surprise when Eli's other hand caressed her leg. She looked down and eyed Eli's one hand stroking Tanner, and she jumped again as she felt Eli's other hand go between her legs, sliding through her moisture. Eli's finger circled her clit a couple of times before he probed deeply into her, eliciting a long groan from both of them. Then he moved his mouth from Tanner to her and licked her clit. One hand stroked Tanner and the other stroked inside Zoë as he kissed and nibbled at her. He stopped for a second to ask, "This okay with you, Tan?" At Tanner's shaky grunt and nod, he went back to sucking Zoë and stroking both of them.

Zoë was in sensory and mental overload and thought she might just burst with pleasure. Her nipples were super-sensitive and her pussy was dripping with arousal. She wanted to close her eyes to the feelings coursing through her, but she also didn't want to miss seeing a thing. She could feel Tanner tensing up next to her and wondered if he felt as crazily reckless as she did, but she forgot about it as the first tingles of an orgasm began spreading through her from deep within her. She grabbed a fistful of Eli's hair and had her arm around Tanner's waist as she groaned in ecstasy with her release. Tanner also gave a long, deep moan, and she could see he was ejaculating all over Eli's hand. They both shook with pleasure. Eli sat back, looking pleased with himself.

"Not bad for a rookie, wouldn't you say? I got a twofer!"

They all cracked up. Their laughter felt almost as good as the orgasms.

Turning serious, Eli regarded Tanner and asked, "Is it alright if I fuck your beautiful wife?"

With his chest still heaving from ecstasy, Tanner looked at Zoë's eager expression and replied with a smile, "Of course it's alright. I can't wait to see it."

Before Eli obliged, he looked concerned for a second. "I don't have any condoms."

Tanner pointed to the cabinet next to the bed and right next to Eli, saying, "Look in there. We have everything you'll need."

Eli opened the cabinet and cocked his head to the side, asking, "Why do you have two different sizes in here? And why do you even need them? Aren't you on birth control, Zoë?"

"I am, Eli. We use those for... special things," she blushed.

Tanner spoke up, "It seems our naughty teacher here is very fond of anal play. We decided it was a good idea to use condoms for that. You know... hygiene and all?"

Eli raised his eyebrows at her and said, "My, my. You *are* the woman of my dreams, Zoë. But why two sizes?"

"Reach behind that bottle of lube," Tanner directed.

Eli complied and pulled out a box of... sex toys. Looking at Zoë with even greater appreciation, he exclaimed, "Ohh... so you like a little mechanical excitement, do you? Well, this is very promising." He rummaged around, randomly pulling out butt plugs, vibrators in a couple of different styles and sizes, a cock ring, and a few things he didn't even understand. "So, you use a condom on this skinny dildo for some backdoor fun? Who gets it in the ass, may I ask?"

In a small voice, Zoë answered, "It's always been me so far, but I've wanted to use it on Tanner too."

Tanner coughed and smiled. "You should have spoken up!" Then he turned his attention back to Eli. "I think for now, we'll stick to the basics. Grab one of the larger condoms and suit up... or not. It's up to Zoë."

Looking serious for a moment, Zoë seemed to consider things. "Look, I know you've only been with Tanner for a long, long time, but Tanner's sister just got pregnant while she was on the pill. It would be one thing for me to have that happen with Tanner, but I'm not sure I'm ready for that with you, Eli, as remote a possibility as it is. So, let's have you use a condom for now, alright?"

Eli smiled and nodded. "It's fine, Zoë. I completely understand. And if that changes, you'll be my first." He gave her a wink.

"Okay," Tanner said encouragingly, "I want to watch you fuck Zoë, Eli. Let's do this!" He rubbed his hands together, chuckling. "This is like my dirtiest fantasy coming to life."

A shiver went through Eli as he tore the package open. He rolled on the condom and lay down on the bed, drawing Zoë down next to him.

Sitting up, Zoë asked sweetly, "Kiss him some more, Tanner, please?" Tanner didn't wait. He lay down beside his friend and brought their mouths together. Immediately, Tanner's hand went for Eli's junk and started to play. Zoë was so turned on she started pulling at her nipples. "God, you guys! You look amazing doing that." She scooched close to Eli and began to caress his body—tentatively at first, then gradually with more confidence. He snaked his arm around her and pulled her on top of him.

Zoë got the picture immediately, so she straddled Eli and let her body sink down onto his erection. The men broke their kiss as Eli hissed and moaned.

Tanner pulled back for a better view. His eyes dilated as he saw his wife impale herself on his best friend's dick as she sighed with pleasure. "Oh my god," he moaned in a strangled voice. "This is so wrong and one hundred percent right at the same time." Tanner reached between Zoë's legs and began to stroke her clit.

Zoë slid up and down on Eli as Eli kept his eyes glued to the action. His moans grew louder and louder, watching Tanner's hand and her pussy gliding up and down.

Tanner scooted into position so that he could use two hands then. Zoe was so turned on and wet, he had no trouble sliding one of his fingers inside of her alongside Eli's shaft. Zoë almost collapsed with desire as she felt the extra stretch and knew that Tanner was caressing both Eli and her at the same time. "Oh, Tanner! You can feel us both, can't you?" she cried. "That is so fucking hot!" Tanner's finger on her clit pushed harder, and she sped up her pumping up and down, clenching her inner muscles on Tanner's hand and Eli's dick, crying, "Yes! Ohh!" as yet another climax rolled through her.

Eli's hips began to thrust upwards over and over, and his eyes slammed shut as if he couldn't handle it anymore. He quickly flipped Zoë over so he was now the one on top. Tanner's hand slipped out of Zoë but he remained next to them, his body plastered to Zoë's and Eli's sides. Tanner stroked Eli's butt with one hand while the other petted and plucked at Zoë's nipple. "Fuck her, Eli! Make Zoë feel you!" His eyes alternated between assessing Zoë's pleasure by the look on her face to the sight of their beautiful bodies joined together. He was getting hard all over again and rubbed his erection against Eli's leg as Eli pumped into Zoë.

Eli pounded harder and faster into Zoë. She moaned and panted with each deep thrust. And finally, he roared with his release. Over and over, he thrust into her, feeling Tanner's firm grip on his ass—until it seemed there was nothing left of him.

Eli collapsed onto Zoë's other side. They all three lay there in post-rapture, stunned silence until Eli asked, "Jesus, did that really just happen?" This brought another purr and a couple of giggles out of Zoë.

"Hmm..." Tanner mused. "You're taking your best man duties pretty seriously, Eli." He laughed with them.

"Just wait until I'm your chief of staff," he responded cockily. Then he grew serious and added, "You both know... this changes everything, right?" He leaned across Zoë to kiss Tanner, and then he moved his mouth to Zoë's. When he'd sufficiently kissed her brains out too, he pulled back and declared, "Now you're both mine... and I'm yours."

"Holy decadence!" breathed Zoë. "We're a throuple!"

After ditching the condom and some general cleanup, they all flopped back onto the bed and slept for three hours.

Chapter Twenty-Three

Zoë awoke when a loud grumbling noise startled her. It sounded really close. As she drifted out of her exhausted slumber fog, she became aware that her head was planted on Eli's belly, and his stomach was growling. So, it was finally hunger that drove them all from their cozy tangle of arms and legs.

She sat up and stretched, taking in the glorious sight of her two men. Their legs were intertwined, and they blinked sleepily at her and at each other.

"I feel like I could eat a horse," Tanner announced. He grabbed his flannel pants and wandered into the kitchen. Two minutes later, he was back, saying, "I just turned on a pot of coffee and put the breakfast casserole in the oven that my assistant made and brought by yesterday. She knew we'd be worn out today, so that was nice of her." Smiling, he eyed Eli and Zoë, who looked like two satisfied cats curled up in the big bed. "It'll be ready soon."

***

After a huge breakfast, Eli got a serious look on his face and said, "Zoë, I need to head over to have a chat with your parents. I think they're planning to go back to the west coast, and I'd frankly prefer to see that happen sooner rather than later. I'm sorry, and I don't want to hurt your feelings in any way, but we need to think of appearances for Tanner's campaign and they don't... um... exactly..." his voice trailed off and he looked at the ceiling with a sigh.

"I get it, Eli. They're embarrassing to me too. Imagine growing up in that house with them." She shook her head. "But I'd like to go over there with you so I can at least spend a little time with them before they leave again. I've barely seen them in years. I feel sort of obligated to play the part of the good daughter, you know?"

"I'll come too," announced Tanner with a resolute expression. "We're family now, for better or worse."

***

A little while later, they all arrived at Zoë's house, where she felt weird watching Eli knock on her own front door. She would have felt even worse walking in on the current residents, however. One never knew...

Zoë's father came to the door looking hungover and grumpy. "Whadaya want, Junior? Oh, hi, Zoë and Mayor Tanner." He made no move to let them through the door.

"May we come in, Dad?" she asked. As her father finally opened the door all the way for them, she asked, "Why did you call Eli 'Junior?'"

Her father guffawed and answered, "Well, yesterday morning he showed up at the door in not much more than skivvies that looked tailor-made, he was wearing a ring worth prob'ly more than this here house, and he's got a snooty sounding name that prob'ly means he's really Elbert Wifflestick, Junior or sumthin'. So, I just cut to the chase and call him Junior."

Eli turned a little pink while Tanner cracked up. Zoë looked lost, so Tanner checked his laughter long enough to explain. "Eli's full name is Elison Whittaker, the Third." He looked at Mr. Deliban and said, "Very perceptive, sir."

"Hah! Called it," the old man chortled. Then he turned around and hollered "Hey, Mariposa! We got company! Git yer skinny ass out here!"

Blanching, Zoë wondered who Mariposa was. Her mother's name was Mildred. But within seconds her mother swanned down the hall toward them in a diaphanous cloud of floaty, tie-dyed material. She had apparently taken her corsage from the wedding and repurposed it, for now she had flowers in her hair. They were looking a bit wilted.

"Hello darlings," she cooed flirtatiously, eyeing Eli up and down. After she licked her lips, she regarded her daughter finally. "Lovely wedding, Zoë. I'm so glad we could do our part."

Blinking and shaking her head slightly, Zoë wondered just what part of the wedding her mother thought she could take credit for. She guessed it was just that her father had managed to walk her down the aisle, so she said nothing to that remark. On closer inspection, both of her parents seemed to be sober, so Zoë thought it would be a good time to clear up a couple of things for once and for all.

She started out with, "Did Dad call you Mariposa?"

"Why, yes, Zoë. Didn't we tell you? We had a spiritual re-awakening when we got to California. We were baptized in the Pacific Ocean by our guru and he anointed us with new names. I am now Mariposa, and your father is now Orion. Aren't they wonderful? I'm forever a butterfly, and your daddy is a constellation and also a hunter." She sighed contentedly.

Zoë privately wondered if her father had ever had the gumption to go out and hunt for anything more challenging than Easter eggs, but she kept her mouth shut about that too. "Yes, lovely names. I'm sure that was a very moving celebration."

"It was damned cold!" Orion exclaimed. "I thought my balls would freeze off. There we were on this nude beach in La Jolla, and the water in the Pacific is colder 'n shit!"

Tanner and Eli seemed to be holding in their snickers, so Zoë forged on. "Sorry to hear about that. I've heard that tourists are often surprised at just how cold the water is there. Anyway," she looked at both her parents solemnly, "now that we're together, I wanted to tell you again how touched and how grateful I was that you used your jackpot money to pay off my student loans and the mortgage on the house. It's been a tremendous relief to me to not be saddled with those payments each month." She hugged her mother and then her father, who both had blank looks on their faces.

"We, uh…" began Mariposa, but Orion gave her a sharp look and pinched her arm. "Ow! What's wrong with you, Otis… er, Orion?"

"You say the mortgage is paid in full?" Orion questioned Zoë with a sneaky expression.

"Well, yes. You paid it off. Mom told me." Looking at her mother, she added, "Didn't you?"

Mariposa seemed to be wrestling with her brain, and then said, "I do recall telling you something about the jackpot."

"What jackpot?" demanded Orion. "Are you holding out on me, woman?"

"No! The one you won in the casino in Reno. You remember," she cajoled her husband.

"That lousy thousand bucks?"

"What?" cried Zoë. "You couldn't have paid off anything with that! Then who paid off the loans?" She spun on Tanner and noticed his face was a little pink, and he was staring at Eli, who was studying his shoes. "Oh. Oh!" She turned back to her parents and said, "Never mind this, but don't go getting any more lousy ideas about mortgaging it again. I've been paying the taxes for years. You left it to me."

"Well, now, honey, that's debatable," said her dad in an oily voice.

Eli broke in and said, "I'm quite sure Zoë could hire a lawyer who'd straighten this all out to everyone's satisfaction. Now, Mr. and Mrs. Deliban, I wanted to come over here today to make sure you two had everything you need for your drive back to California..."

"Where's the rest of our money?" Orion demanded.

"What money?" asked Zoë and Mariposa at the same time.

Smiling politely, Eli explained, "I offered your parents an incentive for them to get back to their 'jobs' in California quickly. It's just a sum that will make sure their van stays in good repair and they don't have any undue stress making the journey."

Orion snorted, and Mariposa squinted at him. "Who's holding out now, you old fool? This Adonis here gave you some money, and you never mentioned it?"

She kept this tirade up for another few minutes until Zoë announced, "Mom, Dad, it was good seeing you. Thanks for making the trip all the way home for the wedding, and I hope you have a safe trip back. Now, if you'll excuse us, we have an appointment we all need to get to. So, when you leave, and I hope that will be *today*, just leave the key under the kitchen doormat." She gave them perfunctory kisses and then marched out the door muttering under her breath. Tanner followed her out and they waited for Eli at the car.

They had to wait a little longer than they expected.

Finally, Eli joined them with a satisfied look on his face. "All set. Let's go home," he said with a grin and a wink.

Once in the car, Zoë asked, "What was all that about?"

"I just let them know that in an hour and a half a certain individual will meet them at the truck stop by the highway entrance. They will exchange the key to the house for the rest of their 'travel money' and some personal property of theirs that they wanted back. I'm sure this will incentivize them to leave right away. Now, who's ready for a *nap*? I find that I'm completely worn out." He winked at Zoë who was staring at him.

Once they were back home, Zoë mentally shook herself. She'd been shocked at the revelation she'd discovered at her old house. Looking from Tanner to Eli, she asked in a hushed voice, "Will you both sit down with me a moment, please?" When they were comfortable on the couch, she went on, "It was you guys all along? You paid all of that money out for me and never said a word? Why?"

Tanner reached for Zoë's face and stroked her cheek lovingly. "It was Eli's doing really. I told him how I was sure you were struggling to make ends meet. I tried as far as I could to get the teachers all better salaries, but I can only do so much. So, Eli swooped in and threw money at the problem as only he can do."

Zoë turned to Eli, and said, "I'm flabbergasted. You didn't even know me, and you did all of that?"

"I did it for Tanner. You'll come to realize that there isn't anything I wouldn't do for him. At that point, you were an extension of him and it made him happier knowing you were taken care of. The money didn't mean much to me, so it was an easy decision. I'm glad I could help. And now that I know you, I'd do it a hundred times over if I had to."

The light went on in Zoë's eyes and she gasped, "You guys had the painters fix up the house too, didn't you? It wasn't that asshole Brandon after all!"

"Hey, don't give assholes a bad name by putting ol' BJ into that category," laughed Tanner. "When I realized he'd led you to believe he'd done something generous for you, I couldn't stand it. I'm just sorry you had to suffer any grief over that creep."

"Why didn't you say something to me? You let me think all of these things happened because of other people."

"Zoë," Tanner explained, "I wasn't trying to buy your love or make you feel in any way that you owed either of us something.

We were concerned with your well-being, and that's what was important. Eli was more than happy to help."

"Well, color me floored. I feel like I've had two guardian angels." She stared at them for a few seconds and then smiled sweetly and thoughtfully. "So, maybe there's *something* I could do to express my gratitude," she suggested.

"I'm completely certain there is," chuckled Eli. "I need to make a couple of calls, and then I'll meet you in bed. Put your heads together and see what you both can come up with." He gave them both a quick kiss and headed to the guest bedroom. He thought of it now as more like his home office because he sure didn't plan to sleep in it.

Chapter Twenty-Four

Eli first contacted a cleaning crew to take care of Zoë's house, and then he called his sister Caro to make some arrangements with her. She would be there in three weeks and was apparently anxious to get started helping out. Caro had plenty of talents he could take advantage of.

One of Caro's first assignments was going to be a makeover for Zoë. Yes, she was gorgeous and polite to everyone she met, but she dressed like... a kindergarten teacher. Plain slacks or skirts with tights and chunky sweaters over bland blouses. She needed to discover her own, more sophisticated style and embrace it. Soon Zoë would look every inch the beautiful young first lady of Kentucky. People would want to look like her, act like her, talk like her. With a little bit of the right packaging, she could become an icon like Jackie Kennedy.

Caro was thrilled by the prospect, and Eli was sure the two of them would become fast friends. At least he hoped. Now he just had to break it to Zoë in a way that didn't sound condescending.

***

That settled, he figured it was time for some relaxation. It was awfully quiet in the master bedroom, and when he opened the door, he discovered why. Tanner and Zoë were naked, wrapped around each other, and sound asleep face to face.

He chuckled, knowing how tired they all still were, pulled off his own clothes, and slipped into bed. The side with the most room was next to Zoë, so he sidled up to her and spooned her. He also reached across her to contact Tanner. Then he too fell asleep with a smile on his face. If this was what the future held for them, he'd be a happy man.

***

Zoë awoke a couple of hours later feeling overly warm. She also felt some things prodding her tummy and her bottom that made her smile. Opening her eyes, she looked at Tanner who was grinning and looking past her. *Oh wow, a girl could get used to this. We'll never even need to turn on the heat with these two guys.*

Zoë felt lips on her shoulder and then the back of her neck. She sighed as Tanner leaned in to kiss her lips. Hands seemed to be roaming all over her body—big, warm masculine hands. Then someone was nibbling her earlobe. It tickled a bit and made her feel all squiggly inside.

"Do we need to figure out what we're doing, you guys, or should we just do what comes naturally?" she asked softly.

"Hmm," mused Eli.

Tanner smiled crookedly and suggested, "Maybe you can tell us about some of the ideas from your 'research' since we're all new to this. Do you have anything that sounded especially decadent and fun? Anything you've fantasized about that you'd like to share with the class?"

Zoë thought for a moment and then excused herself, slipping out from between the two men. She grabbed her Kindle and scrolled through her library. "Aha. Here it is," she muttered to herself. "Now, let me find the scene." She scrolled some more and then her eyes lit up. "Okay, this has always been one of my favorites, but it takes some imagination to figure out just how it physically happens." She handed it to Tanner, and Eli scooted over so the guys could read it together.

"Oh!" Eli exclaimed. "Wow... Oh, I like the idea of that!" He looked up at Zoë who was chewing her lip and turning a little pink. "So, I get how you fit in, Zoë, but, Tanner, which one do you want to be?" he asked with a little laugh.

Tanner, whose breathing seemed to be speeding up, pointed to a passage and announced, "Oh, I'd like to do what this guy is doing right there." He turned to Zoë, asking, "You ready for this?"

Her eyes were dilated, and she was already reaching for their bottle of lube to give to Eli. "So ready." Then she pulled the blankets down so no one would get caught up in them. She looked at Eli and asked, "Can I watch you get Tanner ready?"

"Not only can you watch, I think you'd enjoy helping." Eli looked at Tanner, "You ready, Tan?"

"Just give me a moment," he answered, hopping out of bed and heading to the bathroom. A few minutes later, he was back with an eager grin in his face. "Where do you want me, Eli?"

"Oh, just lie down and get comfortable," Eli answered, popping open the bottle of lube. Then he told Zoë, "Spread his ass cheeks open."

"Oh, God," she muttered as she grabbed her husband's butt. She pulled him open and watched as Eli poured some lube onto Tanner's hole. "I can't believe this," she said as if to herself.

"OK, now take one of your fingers and start massaging the lube around the opening," Eli coaxed. "Good, that's it. I'm sure he's glad you keep your nails short. Okay, a little more lube." He dribbled some more on Tanner and then said, "Now give me your hand." He coated her finger with lube. "Alright, now press on him gently and slowly. When he relaxes enough, you can start pushing inside."

Tanner began to squirm. He was used to Eli and his ministrations, but this show and tell version was making him all hot and bothered like never before. He could already feel his erection throbbing beneath him. When Zoë's thin finger broke the barrier of his ring of muscles, he let out a long groan.

"Is it okay? Are you alright, Tanner?" she asked nervously.

Tanner just laughed with a little choking groan thrown in.

Eli answered for him, "Believe me—he's fine. That was a happy sound. Okay, you're doing great, Zoë. Now let me give you a little more lube, and we'll have you use two fingers."

"Ohh... this is so... I don't even know." She shuddered. "I feel so naughty!" She pulled her finger almost all the way out and then pushed in again with a second finger. Tanner groaned as his cheek muscles squeezed and released.

Eli chuckled and squirted some more. Then he greased up his own finger and slowly slid it inside Tanner along with Zoë's fingers.

Tanner made a long, muffled sound into the pillow. Then he jumped as Eli's finger rubbed his prostate. "Ahh!"

"See that?" Eli asked. "That's the magic button. If you can hit that when he comes, look out! He'll erupt like a volcano."

"Wow," she breathed. "That's pretty amazing."

In a strangled voice, Tanner finally spoke up intelligibly, "Okay, y'all. Better quit now. I'm ready as I'll ever be, and I need to stay that way for Zoë." He groaned again long and hard as they slowly removed their fingers. Taking charge, Tanner sat up and directed Zoë to lie back on the bed with her legs over the edge. "Sit like that, honey. Good, now spread your legs. Eli, do you want to get her ready for me?" Tanner stood up next to Eli.

"My pleasure," Eli answered, dropping to his knees between her legs. He kissed her inner thighs and then covered her mound with his mouth. His tongue expertly probed her clit, making her writhe within moments. Pulling back for a moment he whispered, "You taste so good, Zoë." Then he dove back down and licked her to a frenzy with his relentless, stiff tongue.

All the while, Tanner stood by stroking his own shaft that gleamed with a drop of precum.

Zoë didn't know where to look. Two beautiful men—one so turned on he was pleasuring himself, and the other with his face buried between her legs. She felt herself getting closer and closer to her own release, and when it came, she finally couldn't keep her eyes open. She panted through spasm after spasm of ecstasy. Eli's mouth left her pussy finally, and a new noise made her eyes pop open again.

Eli, still on his knees, was sucking Tanner. "Oh, God that's hot," she moaned once again as her hand moved involuntarily to her clit. She couldn't help it; she needed friction as she watched all of that sexy male beauty.

Tanner gently pulled away from Eli and traded places with him between Zoë's legs. As Eli reached for a condom, Tanner shoved himself into Zoë. She was drenched with Eli's saliva and her own arousal, so he slid right in.

Eli noticed that Tanner had to bend his knees to keep fucking Zoë, so he grabbed a couple of pillows. "Hang on a sec, you two," he ordered and then slipped the pillows under Zoë's butt. "There. That's better. Are you okay, Zoë?"

"Ye....esssss," she sighed as Tanner drove home inside her again. She watched, transfixed, as Eli lubed up his sheathed erection. When Eli stepped behind Tanner and began to kiss Tanner's neck, she pushed harder with the fingers on her clit. She'd never been so turned on... ever. Stroking herself as Tanner's pulsing cock shoved in and out of her, she made purring, moaning noises.

Zoë watched intently as one of Eli's hands disappeared behind Tanner a moment. It was clear that he was guiding himself into Tanner when her husband's eyes closed in bliss and his head fell back a bit. Tanner's chest heaved, but he kept up his thrusting motion in and out of Zoë. Only now, the thrusts were harder and deeper as if propelled from behind as Eli pushed in and out of Tanner.

Eli gripped Tanner's hips with so much force, his fingertips turned white. He kissed Tanner's neck and then bit down on his earlobe and sucked into his mouth.

Zoë was beside herself. To see Tanner giving and receiving pleasure like this was incredible—beyond hotness.

Tanner replaced her hand on her pussy with his own, and he stroked it in time with Eli's thrusts that propelled him into Zoë. He stopped stroking then and pinched her clit between his fingers with a firm grip.

Harder, faster, deeper—Eli fucked Tanner's ass and Tanner fucked Zoë until, "Ohhhhnnnn," she moaned.

She watched spellbound as every muscle in Tanner's body seemed to stiffen while he followed her in climax, hollering out his release. "Ahhhhholy fuck!"

Growling, Eli gave a few more ferocious thrusts into Tanner and then he too growled out a primal outcry as he came with his eyes squeezed shut. Within seconds, they melted into a satisfied, sweaty mass of bodies on the bed.

"Can I just say, y'all, that that was the most astounding ex-perience of my life?" Tanner asked in an incredulous tone.

"Me too," agreed Zoë. "Transcendental."

Eli chuckled, "Mm-hmm," and asked, "What's next on your menu, Zoë honey? That one's going to be hard to top." He kissed Zoë as she giggled and then Tanner. Looking serious, he added, "Thank you both for including me. Just yesterday I was sure I'd lost everything, and now I have more than I could have ever imagined."

"I know just what you mean, Eli," Tanner said softly as he stroked Eli's jaw. "And just wait until both of you take a turn as the one in the middle. I don't, for once, even have words to describe how unbelievable it is. I love you both so much."

Eli smiled at them and asked, "Is the shower big enough for a throuple?"

Chapter Twenty-Five

The next days were a whirlwind of activity. Eli had Tanner booked for plenty of speaking engagements, beginning with local television and radio stations around Kentucky. As his popularity grew, the size of his audience would also grow. Tanner was a natural in front of a microphone or a camera. His deep, well-modulated voice captured listeners who hung on every last word when he answered the questions posed by radio talk show hosts. And when he sat for television interviews, everyone was attracted to such a ridiculously handsome young man. He had a way of making his audience feel special just by association, and his reputation for putting Honeybee Hollow on the map did wonders for his popularity.

Tanner also had a knack for answering tough questions in a way that made the interviewer comfortable and the listeners convinced he had their best interests at heart. He was never argumentative and showed that he had a good sense of humor. He was a born leader who had a deep love for the great commonwealth of Kentucky. The number of his loyal supporters grew and grew each time he made an appearance.

***

Zoë didn't have a lot of time yet to help out because she was both busy teaching her kindergarten classes—one in the morning and one in the afternoon—and working with Caro who'd swooped in with strong ideas about image building.

Tanner let the ladies both know that he didn't want Zoë to feel she needed to change herself. Some designer clothes would be fine, but she already knew how to speak and comport herself around any sort of folks.

Eli agreed—Zoë was perfect. It was just her wardrobe that needed a major overhaul. He thought of how elegant she'd looked as a bride and looked forward to seeing her decked out for formal occasions in the future. "Just think of the new wardrobe," he told them, "as an extra wedding gift." He had a feeling he'd enjoy it every bit as much as Zoë.

Because his curiosity was killing him, Eli finally asked Tanner, "How did Zoë turn out so normal with such nutty parents raising her?"

Tanner's answer was, "Probably because she spent a lot of time at our house growing up. She and Madison were inseparable friends, and our parents let Zoë know she was always welcome at our table. I think fairly often her parents were neglectful regarding meals and basic necessities. From a very young age, I think Zoë felt closer to my parents than to her own sometimes. She also spent a lot of time in the library reading, and my mama made sure she read everything she had Madison and me read as kids. Mama always said she wanted our heads filled with the right stuff." He smiled at that, thinking how Mama might get a laugh out of Zoë's choice of reading material these days. Then again, his mother probably loved reading that stuff too. She had pretty eclectic tastes when it came to literature.

The first weekend that Caro was in town, the two ladies headed up to Louisville to do some serious shopping. Madison had clued Zoë in about shopping at one of the greatest boutiques you could ever hope to find. Located next door to her Madison Hatter milliner shop, the boutique called Spice had a reputation for trend-setting fashion and elegant designs for all occasions. Zoë had actually met the owners of the shop when Madison and Halden got married, and she liked all of the ladies.

Madison let them know at Spice that her sister-in-law would be coming and had some serious clothing needs and virtually an unlimited budget. She was also drop-dead gorgeous, so the ladies of Spice couldn't wait to dress her.

And dress her, they did. From the inside out. Molly, the original owner and founder of the boutique, saw to it that Zoë now had an exquisite lingerie wardrobe because nothing gave a woman more confidence and made her feel more elegant, she explained, than incredible lingerie. Amelia, their custom designer, delighted in outfitting Zoë in day and nighttime fashions befitting the wife of a soon-to-be governor. Åse, their partner and jewelry designer, suggested accessories to go with Amelia's amazing designs. They recommended a trendy shoe store a block away called Walk This Way where Zoë picked up a delightful collection of shoes and boots. And because it was still winter and quite chilly, she topped off her outfits with some great hats from Madison Hatter.

Exhausted after a long day of shopping, Zoë and Caro retired to the presidential suite at the Grand Walton Hotel in downtown Louisville. Zoë was taken aback by the accommodations.

"I've never stayed in a place like this," she exclaimed to Caro when they arrived upstairs. It was an opulently appointed suite with a large parlor connecting two enormous bedrooms. "This is amazing." Fresh flowers and a large basket of fruit sat on the glass coffee table.

Caro trilled a laugh, "You better get used to it, Zoë. You're going to be seeing this kind of thing more and more as Tanner's career advances."

"I guess so," Zoë said wistfully. "I just hope I don't disappoint him somehow."

Shaking her head, Caro was quick to offer, "Tanner's so crazy about you, you could never disappoint him. And besides, I think you'll make an incredible first lady."

"You mean of Kentucky, right?"

"I mean first lady, as in wife of the president one day," Caro stated as she flopped on the couch and kicked off her shoes. "So, do you want to have room service sent up, or would you rather go out for dinner? I understand the food here is fantastic."

Sighing, Zoë answered, "If it's all the same to you, room service sounds wonderful. I'd like to put on some comfy clothes and slippers and just forget to be a lady for a while. In fact, I think I'll go take a shower, and then we can look at the menu. Is that alright with you?"

"Sounds perfect. You're a woman after my own heart."

After showers and an exquisite supper, they poured some wine and curled up in the large, comfy couch.

"You know, Zoë, you can send my brother back to your old house to live with me. You don't have to let him stay with you and Tanner indefinitely if you'd like your privacy," Caro said as she looked closely at Zoë's face. "I know life in the public eye is bound to get to you eventually, and being newlyweds might make that extra difficult. So, feel free to boot him out when you and Tanner need alone time."

Not knowing what to say, Zoë took a sip of wine and tried to control the deep red blush that had just overtaken her face. It didn't work.

Looking at Zoë shrewdly, Caro nodded imperceptibly and said quietly, "I know about them."

"What?" Zoë's eyes popped. "Who?"

"Come on Zoë. You can't be blind. I know my brother's been in love with Tanner for years. I know why he hasn't dated, and I know he still feels that way." She studied Zoë's face for any sign of shock, but only picked up on embarrassment.

"How did you know?" Zoë asked, confirming that this was no revelation to her either.

"Tanner used to join us in the Hamptons for spring break. He and Eli were inseparable, as much as my mother tried to foist me off on Tanner. That never worked. It embarrassed me no end when she tried to do her matchmaking. Don't get me wrong, I was definitely attracted to Tanner. Who wouldn't be?" she asked with a smile. "But one day, I took a walk on the beach and came across a protected cove that not too many people knew about. It was a great place to go and meditate or whatever, but that day when I got there, it was already occupied. Eli and Tanner were sitting way in the back of the cove, and they were close to each other. Closer than two buddies normally sit. And they were holding hands. That's all, but the air of intimacy around them was so intense, I just knew that they were more than just roommates." She paused a second to sip her wine. "They didn't see me, and I was glad about that because I didn't want Tanner to be uncomfortable. I knew Eli was bi. He'd told me years before that."

"Oh," Zoë said on a long exhale. "I... um... don't know what to say to that." Zoë stared intently at her goblet of wine.

"I also know Eli is crazy about you."

Zoë's eyes flew to Caro, and she looked nervous.

"Look, Zoë, I'm not making any judgment here. You may have heard that I spent a few of my 'formative years' touring with a rock band when I should have been finishing my degree. So... you might say that I have been known to, um, *dabble* in a few escapades that were pretty exciting—and I'm not referring to drugs. So, if—or when—you decide to take things to a new level with Tanner and Eli, you'll get no criticism from me. I say, go girl!"

Zoë let out a relieved breath. "Too late. It's a done deal." She gave Caro a shy smile.

"Alright, Zoë," Caro laughed. "Just be careful. If the public ever got wind of it—look out!" With a broad smile, she asked, "How do you feel about Eli? Sorry to be so nosy. I can't help myself."

"I think Eli is a terrific guy. It pissed me off that they took a while to level with me, but once the shock wore off, I realized I could never be the one to break them apart. Eli felt that way about Tanner and me as well. So, now that we've decided to try being a throuple... that's such a silly word," she said with a laugh, "I feel like we all somehow complete each other. Am I making any sense, or do I sound like a corny movie?"

"I get it." Caro said with a nod.

"And oh, God, together?" Zoë continued, "hotter than blue blazes!" She blushed again. "Just shut me up. I shouldn't even talk about this."

"Do you mind if I ask something personal?"

Zoë laughed, "How do we get more personal?"

Leveling Zoë with a thoughtful look, Caro wondered out loud, "What do you think the guys are doing with you here and them at home? Does that bother you? Wait. You don't need to answer that." Caro looked down at her lap. "I can be awfully forward, I'm afraid."

With a serious expression, Zoë answered, "Honestly, it's been a long time since I've been able to confide in anyone —well, another woman anyway—now that Madison lives in Louisville. I don't mind the probing questions, especially since I understand you have our best interests at heart. You were as kind as can be to drop everything to come down to Podunk, USA to help out a country boy and his bumpkin wife turn into respectable people."

"I did nothing of the sort," laughed Caro. "You're both wonderful people, and all you needed was a little fancy packaging. I know you're going to have people eating from the palm of your hand. I adore Tanner, and when I met you, I knew you were someone very special. I also love my brother and wanted to be a part of what he knows is going to be a big deal. I decided that instead of letting the freight train run over me, I'd hop on and hitch a ride."

"Such an appropriate analogy for life with those two. Tanner has all the ambition in the world and has the charisma to match it, and Eli has the power and the knowhow to get things accomplished." Zoë stayed quiet for a moment, clearly pondering her next statement. "So," she said with a sigh, "we've talked about just what you've asked. What do we do when two of us are together and the other can't be there for one reason or another?" She sipped her wine again and continued. "We have made the promise to be one hundred percent exclusive—that goes without saying, and we're careful with each other's feelings at all times. I don't mind if Tanner and Eli are intimate when I'm not there, and Eli is obviously fine with Tanner and me being intimate since we're the married couple," she laughed softly. "Tanner says he will be fine knowing that Eli and I may want to be intimate if he's not around, but that's going to take me a while to adjust to. We need to build on our relationship first. Does that sound crazy? I've done plenty of... um... stuff with the two of them together, so I ought to feel as comfortable as can be with Eli. It's just going to take us a little bit of time, I think."

"I understand that. There are many ways to be intimate with someone," Caro said with a slow nod. "And I have no doubt you'll get there. I just have to worry a little about Eli. He's the most wonderful brother and he's so loving, I'd hate for anything to happen so that he ends up getting hurt."

Zoë smiled gently, "I know. It was gut-wrenching to see what kind of agony he was in after the wedding. I'd do anything in my power before letting that happen again. Eli was trying so hard to do the right thing, and it was killing him. And I guess

Tanner has had similar trouble dealing with the possibility of losing one of us as well. So, believe me, we're going to be very, very careful with each other's hearts."

"May I ask, Zoë, why did it take so long for you and Tanner to get back together? I understand you were high school sweethearts."

Zoë got a flat look in her eye and said, "First, *he* wanted a clean break. That broke my heart, and I was too pissed off to listen to him when he wanted to try again. Then, as I became aware that he had such lofty political ambitions, I wanted to stay as far away as possible from him."

"You dislike politics that much?" Caro asked with surprise.

"Not at all. I think it's exciting." Zoë's eyes lit up. "I was afraid I'd slow him down or bring him down in some way. I'm a kindergarten teacher from nowhere who was raised by wolves," she laughed. "I thought he needed someone more polished and sophisticated. Probably someone like you, actually."

"Hah! Yeah, well, that didn't exactly work out, did it?" Caro laughed. "Don't sell yourself short, Zoë. I think, Eli thinks, and obviously Tanner thinks you're perfect the way you are. And I'm also not so polished since my reputation was tarnished years ago." She swallowed the last of her wine and gave Zoë a funny look, "I'm freaking jealous of you, lucky bitch! Where's that bottle? I need another glass of wine."

They both laughed at that.

"Since we're getting down and dirty," Caro explained in a droll tone, "I have to say that although I've definitely partaken in ménage sex, it was more just experimentation. It was fun—and hotter than hell—but I can imagine how much better it would be if all participants had strong feelings for one another. That has to be a whole new level of... wow."

"Yeah," breathed Zoë. "I'd read about it and that was titillating, but actually *experiencing* it with Tanner and Eli is mind-blowing."

Changing her tone to a more serious one Caro said, "Zoë, if you all need any help or just to talk, I'm here for you, alright?" She sloshed some more wine in her glass, but Zoë indicated she was fine with hers. "I like you and I think it's going to be a blast being part of the Eli, Tanner, Zoë Team. Instead of Kentucky's Power Couple, you'll be the Power Throuple! We just need to keep the reality of it quiet. For now, anyway."

"Caro, I'm so happy you came to town."

Chapter Twenty-Six

The next day they had a brunch in the hotel and then hit some larger stores where they bought Zoë a couple of jackets and coats and browsed the spring collections. They didn't like the high-end boutique sections of the department stores anywhere nearly as much as what they'd seen at Spice, so they congratulated themselves on going there first.

Zoë was glad they'd ridden over in a limo so there was enough room for all the bags and boxes they dragged back to Honeybee Hollow. Caro told her to ignore all of the price tags because everything was to be Eli's gift, and he had almost as much money as Mark Zuckerberg, but every so often Zoë caught a glimpse of one and it gave her heart palpitations.

The next project Caro planned to take on with Zoë was to add some highlights to Zoë's dark hair and have a stylist work with her on makeup tricks. She had her favorites flown in from New York.

The general idea for Zoë was to create a look for her that said sophisticated and still approachable. So, they kept her makeup light and her hair long, thus giving her a youthful appearance, but the fashions were a little edgier. She had to look appropriate next to her gorgeous husband who'd adapted a similar appearance. Eli also flew in a crew for Tanner, and his clothes were all custom tailored, but he never looked stuffy or uncomfortable. He had to look right speaking to a group of farmers as well as to businessmen and investors.

All of that would happen over the next week, but for now, Zoë was anxious to get back to The Hollow. She wanted to see her men. The trip home in the limo took hours, and they spent the time having dinner that they'd picked up on their way out of Louisville and just chatting about whatever popped into their heads.

Except for the porch light and a small lamp in the living room, the house looked dark and silent when the limo driver dropped her off and helped her in with her mountain of packages. So, Zoë thanked the guy, left everything in a pile near the front door, and went in search of intelligent life in the house.

The light from the television was all Zoë could see as she made her way down the hall, but there wasn't a single sound.

In the big bed, Eli sat watching television with headphones on, and Tanner lay curled up beside him, sound asleep. Looking up, Eli broke into a beaming smile and pulled off the headphones. He put his fingers to his lips in a silencing gesture and then slid out of bed without a stitch on.

As if he did it every day, Eli reached for Zoë and enveloped her in a big, warm, naked hug. "Welcome home," he greeted her in a whisper. "Did you have a good time with my sister?"

With a happy smile, Zoë answered, "We had a great time and found lots of terrific things. I can't thank you enough, Eli. Really."

"My pleasure. Do you need some help with packages?" he asked pulling back and looking at her.

Zoë smiled and replied quietly, "That would be great. Do you want to grab some clothes first?" She looked pointedly down— Eli was *very* happy to see her.

"Eh," he said with a shrug then winked at her and went on quietly, "Let's grab your stuff and you can tell me all about your trip with Caro." Then he hugged her again, kissing her cheek, and reached around to pick up his jeans off the floor. Once he was semi-dressed—commando she noticed—he flicked off the television.

When they got to the front door where all the packages lay, Eli chuckled. "Did you two ladies leave anything in Louisville? I don't know if this stuff is even going to all fit in the closet, so why don't we put it in the guest room and sort things out tomorrow when Tanner's conscious? I don't want to wake him up."

"Sounds good. Is he pretty worn out?" Zoë asked with concern.

Eli smiled sweetly. "He's had a long week. Just today he had to give three speeches and then there was a rally for him over in Middlesboro. "Don't worry, Zoë. He lives for this stuff. Feel like having a drink with me?"

"That sounds lovely," she answered, so they headed for the kitchen where he poured them both glasses of chilled, white wine, and then took their glasses to the living room. As they sat down on the couch, Eli scooted her toward him and wrapped his arm around her. "This is nice, Eli," she said with a sigh as she relaxed against his warm body. She had an immediate desire to nuzzle his bare chest with her face and soak in some of his deliciousness. She held back, though, for the time being.

"So, have you had the chance yet to watch Tanner create his magic in front of a crowd?" Eli asked as he stroked her arm and toyed with her hair.

Resisting the urge to purr, she answered, "Only on a small scale. I've watched him in town meetings. Sometimes people come in with a chip on their shoulder about some real or perceived wrong, and he can not only defuse the situation, he makes everyone feel important and... well, listened to. He's settled disputes and made all attendees feel like a part of the decision-making process. It's incredible to watch his King

Solomon approach to justice and management. I've been so proud of him."

"And yet you avoided him for years, Zoë. How could you?"

She bristled at that question. "I had to. For my own preservation. I thought he needed to go places with someone more like Caro who knows the ropes on how to behave and how to look. I was raised by goofball hippies, remember? I didn't want to be Tanner's downfall."

"Oh, Zoë. You have no idea how much that man loves you. You could never be his downfall. You're perfect just the way you are."

Looking down rather than at him, she asked, "What if we're both his downfall, though? What if his love for both of us keeps him from achieving his dream? The public won't accept us the way we are; you know it and I know it." Finally, she looked Eli in the eye. "As much as I love this, if we're found out, he'll be ruined."

"Are you telling me I need to back away? Is that what you want?" he asked in a sad voice. "Because you know I will. I love him that much. I told him a long time ago I'd be content if all we could be is best friends. That's not completely accurate, but I could learn to adjust if I had to."

"No, Eli. I'm not asking that at all. I don't want any one of us to lead a half-life. I'm already incredibly fond of you, and losing you would be awful. I'm just saying that your sister has already figured us out, and it may just be a matter of time before someone else does who has more to gain by spreading the news."

Sighing, Eli pondered what Zoë said. It definitely worried him. "We'll just have to be extra careful then." He thought a few seconds and added, "Back to your perceived notion that you're somehow less than what Tanner needs where he's headed, I'm sure you didn't see what I saw at your wedding."

Zoë blinked and asked, "What was that?"

Pulling her closer, he went on, "I saw men all over the reception looking at you like they wanted you. They envy the hell out of Tanner because you married him. Women looked at you with admiration. I, quite honestly, expected some jealously from them, but the fact that you make everyone around you feel so comfortable says a lot for your character and how people will continue to respond to you. Tanner told me years ago he's loved you since you were little kids, and he never stopped. I think, in his very perceptive way even back then, he saw what is so special about you. I see it, Zoë. You're an amazing woman. You look people in the eye when you speak to them and make them feel special."

Laughing, Zoë pointed out, "It comes from working with five-year-olds all day, no doubt."

"Well, never lose it. I'm falling for you just as hard as Tanner did."

Zoë sucked in a tiny breath, "Oh!"

Eli carefully took her wineglass and set it on the coffee table next to his, and then leaned in to kiss her. It was a gentle, sweet kiss that underscored his words. He really was falling for her. Zoë slipped her arms around his neck then and tilted her head for better access. Their kisses grew deeper and more possessive. Finally, they broke apart and Zoë asked out of the blue, "Did you and Tanner have sex while I was gone?"

Laughing, Eli answered, "We're two horny young men who are crazy about each other. What do you think?"

"I think I'm happy about that. Can you tell me what you did?"

Eli pulled back and looked her in the eye. "So, what we do turns you on that much? You need to hear about it?"

"Yes." She couldn't help squirming a little.

"Okay," he said with a deep breath. "Earlier tonight, I sucked him for a while and then fucked his ass. He came—and then basically passed out while I was in the shower."

Zoë squeezed her legs together and blushed. She could feel her arousal as she conjured up the picture of that in her head. "What about yesterday?" She boldly reached into Eli's pants and discovered that talking about this was making him hard as well.

"He fucked me," he said with a groan. "Keep doing that with your hand. It feels so good."

"Do you want to fuck me? I'm so turned on right now, you have no idea."

Eli sighed, "Yes. More than anything. I need a condom, though."

"Oh, screw the condoms. The pill works for most people." Zoë stood and pulled off her pants and undies. Then she knelt in front of Eli who'd undone his jeans and shoved them down. She leaned over him and grasped his erection, sliding him into her mouth at the same time.

Eli closed his eyes and leaned his head back. He groaned with pleasure as Zoë sucked on him, sliding her hand up and down in time with her mouth. After a couple of minutes of bliss, he announced, "That's enough. Stand up and turn around."

So, Zoë pulled back, letting go of him with a satisfying pop and quickly turned around. She started to back onto Eli's lap, but he stopped her by grasping her hips. "Bend over," he ordered, eyeing her luscious bottom.

Zoë did as she was told and gasped loudly with surprise as Eli buried his face in her from behind. This was a completely new sensation she'd never experienced, and it seemed dirty and naughty and incredibly wonderful. She could feel his nose prodding her as he licked from front to back. Her legs began to shake, and she vibrated with Eli's chuckle as he probed and tasted her with his tongue.

"God, I love the way you taste. I could do this forever," he told her between licks. "But I need to fuck you so badly. Sit on my dick."

Zoë was almost sad to quit the wonderful tongue action he was giving her, but she was also anxious for more, so she guided him inside as she lowered herself down. She moaned loudly with a tremendous shudder, "Oh, Eli, you feel so good like this."

As she leaned back onto his chest, he reached around and located her clit with his fingers. "God, it feels incredible being inside you bare. It's amazing." He was beginning to create some wonderful friction for her with his dick and his hand when the atmosphere in the room changed suddenly.

"Y'all mind if I join the party? It looks like you're having fun out here," Tanner asked a little shyly. "I got lonely and then thought I heard your voices." He stood there in nothing but his glorious birthday suit, tugging at his erection.

Zoë looked into her husband's eyes and stated, "Eli is inside me bare, Tanner, and it feels sooo good. He also used his mouth on me in an incredible way." She ended with a wanton groan. She continued to rise and fall on Eli's lap. "Do you want me to make you feel good too?"

Tanner gave a strangled moan and yanked harder on his boner.

Zoë reached for him as he stepped closer to the couch, and she leaned forward. She pulled him to her mouth and began to fellate Tanner while Eli ground up into her from below.

Eli kept a firm grasp on Zoë's hip with one hand as the other continued to prod, swirl, and pinch at her firm nub. She was so aroused; she could feel how ultra-sensitized she was. Her clit seemed twice its normal size.

As she leaned into Tanner, he supported her by grasping her shoulders. She wanted to be careful with her mouth as she ground up and down against Eli. After a couple of minutes of listening to both men gasp and moan in pleasure, she felt herself beginning to come. Her thighs tensed and burned as the familiar warmth spread through her body, and the spasms of her orgasm took over. No sooner had she begun to shake when her mouth filled with Tanner's release as he made a long, guttural noise. She swallowed and swallowed, breathing raggedly through her nose.

"Oh my God, you two!" cried Eli, as he then smashed Zoë's hips against his body. He was so deep inside her; she felt his orgasm trigger more spasms of her own.

Tanner slid from her mouth and dropped to his knees in front of her. He wrapped his arms around Zoë and kissed her hungrily, tasting his own seed on her tongue. He also reached one hand beyond Zoë, and wrapped it around Eli's head. "I love you both so much. How did I ever get to be so lucky?" He thought for a minute and then asked, "Eli, are you really inside our beautiful Zoë bare?"

Zoë giggled, and Eli answered, "I am. She loves me now, so it's alright." Her head whipped around to look at him, and he winked at her.

"Cool," said Tanner with a sleepy smile. "That's great news."

Chapter Twenty-Seven

During the months leading up to the state primary elections, life was hectic for all three of them. Eli was in his element, overseeing the campaign workers and arranging interviews and events for Tanner to attend and wow people with his charisma. Tanner had to reel Eli in now and then, however. Eli's enthusiasm for getting Tanner elected tended to blind him to the fact that Tanner still had a job to do as mayor, and that needed to take up a good portion of his time. Nevertheless, there was a buzz of excitement in the small town whose residents were all proud of the impressive young man they'd watched grow up and now had a real shot at the highest job in the state.

In late May, Zoë had to make a difficult decision. The principal of her school wanted to know Zoë's plans for the next year. Should Tanner possibly lose the election, she certainly didn't want to stop teaching, but if he did win, she didn't want to quit midyear and disrupt things for the children either. As a compromise, they decided she could delay her decision at least until the primary was over, but the principal already had someone else in mind for her job and didn't want to lose that teacher to another school district.

So, throughout the rest of the winter and into spring, Tanner and Zoë led a strange existence. During the day, they went to their respective jobs and tried to be as normal as possible. In the evenings, they often got dressed up and headed off to fundraising or other political rallies and functions. They hob-nobbed with the elite moneyed folks in Kentucky, smiling and saying all of the perfect words.

Zoë was a natural at it, no matter how many misgivings she'd had about her ability to fit in. Eli was right; she dazzled people. Men lusted, women either envied or copied, but in all cases, they took notice of the charming young school teacher who was obviously deeply in love with her dashingly handsome and eloquent husband. They were the ultimate couple.

Many weekends found them touring farms and ranches around the state as well. Tanner had grown up around his father's customers, many of whom were horse owners, so he managed to fit right in with them as easily as the people they met at fancier occasions. Tanner and Zoë both admired acres and acres of cornfields, patted horses, cattle, and even a few pigs here and there. They shook what must have been millions of hands and smiled until their cheeks ached.

All the while, Eli stayed in the background, bursting with pride for the two people he loved so dearly—for he and Zoë had declared their love for one another as much as they both loved Tanner. He watched as Kentuckians were drawn to Tanner and Zoë. He observed as they spoke to people and analyzed who unconsciously mirrored their movements and gestures—a dead giveaway as to what they felt. When someone had a more reserved or negative reaction to the couple, either Eli or Caro would casually seek them out and carefully discover the source of their negativity. Sometimes they could just discuss the problem on the spot and clear things up, or other times, Eli would discuss issues with Tanner that would later be ad-dressed in a public speech or a future debate. Eli didn't want to leave anything to chance.

Caro's job was to find out as much as she could about Tan-ner's opposition. It was a pretty easy job coming up to the pri-mary, however, because in the face of Tanner's huge popularity, one by one, the other candidates fell by the wayside, leaving him with just one challenger for his party's nomination. When that guy's reputation was blown two weeks before the election, he too would have thrown in the towel, except that it was too late. Some resourceful photographer took photos of the man leaving an AA meeting and then later the same day shoplifting a bottle of scotch from a local liquor store. People didn't know whether to be sorry for the guy because he was overstressed, mad about his stealing, or infuriated at him for being a scotch drinker in Kentucky. Bourbon was like the state beverage in a commonwealth that produced ninety-five percent of the bourbon that is consumed worldwide. In any case, his shot at winning the nomination went kablooey with that magnificent faux pas.

Once the party nomination seemed in the bag, Caro turned her focus to the opposing party's candidates. There would be no incumbent this year, so she felt they were on a level playing field, at least. She had her eye on one guy in particular who seemed ready to clinch the party's nomination and wondered what his story would be. She intended to find out.

What she found was a rich guy with a bunch of wealthy friends, not much personality or experience, but he looked good in a suit for a fifty-year-old man. His name was Terrence Backman, and he seemed full of fluff to her. He had the look of a man who spent many an hour on the golf course, but he was pleasant.

***

At night, after all of the work, speeches, glad-handing and general being out in the public eye was finished for the day, they would all retire to the mayor's house for a nightcap. Caro usually stayed long enough to be friendly but not so long that she felt like an intruder. She knew they were all exhausted.

And they were. Each night, usually depending on who was the most worn out, that person would end up in bed first, and the other two would just climb in on either side as they wore out. There was never any side of the bed possessiveness. They all slept in the nude, and it often resembled a pile of arms and legs crisscrossing haphazardly around each other. They were all three snugglers, so personal space barely existed for them. If they didn't make love when they first got to bed, they usually managed to wake each other up at some point during the night to do so. Each was secure in the strength of their unusual union. Eli may have preferred his more anonymous role in the grand plan, but he was every bit as important to their success as the other two and an equal partner in the bedroom.

***

Finally, on a Tuesday in late June, they were not the least bit surprised when Tanner locked in the nomination for his party's choice to be the Governor of Kentucky. A few people thought he was just too young and inexperienced for the job, but the press continued to highlight his many accomplishments as mayor of Honeybee Hollow, so those doubters were usually shot down pretty quickly by people accusing them of reverse ageism.

Zoë quit her job. It was a sad day for her as she loved her classroom and everything about her career as a teacher. But she loved Tanner even more, and he would need her by his side throughout the rest of the campaign. He was no shoo-in for the governorship. It was going to be a bloody battle ahead for them.

Tanner had already worked so hard to get the nomination, and now, as Eli put it, "The real work begins."

So, Zoë moved out of the school room and into the campaign headquarters where she could help Eli. And when she wasn't busy making phone calls or running around, she gave talks to ladies' auxiliaries, garden clubs, book clubs, church groups, and anywhere they thought she could make a difference. She found she was beginning to enjoy speaking to large groups of adults instead of five-year-olds after all. She was a wonderful representative for her husband.

Chapter Twenty-Eight

In July, Tanner's office got a call from someone who claimed to be the executive assistant to someone she referred to as Colonel. Apparently, this Colonel wanted a meeting immediately with Mayor Lassiter. The assistant let Tanner's assistant Opal know that Colonel got what he wanted when he wanted it, and the meeting was to be at seven o'clock Saturday morning aboard Colonel's private fishing boat on the Cumberland River, and Tanner was directed to come prepared to fish. Directions to the marina were sent via email as they spoke.

Needless to say, when Tanner got the message, he laughed.

"What kind of a jerk calls himself Colonel in Kentucky? Colonel who? Did she happen to say what he's the colonel of?" he asked Opal, whose face had gone red. "And that area is over two hours away by car. Is he nuts or something?"

"Sorry, Mayor Lassiter, I'm just relaying the information. She wouldn't stay on the line long enough for me to ask any questions for you. The only other information she gave me was that he wanted to discuss your campaign." Opal looked guilty, so Tanner tried to put her mind at ease.

"I'm not upset with you, Opal. Get her back on the line, please, and tell her my weekend is already booked up completely. I have no intention of getting up before dawn to go fishing with some cocky crackpot. And try to figure out what this is all about while you're at it." As soon as Opal left his office, Tanner phoned Eli.

"Have you ever heard of anyone in Kentucky called Colonel?" he asked without preamble.

Not missing a beat, Eli quipped, "No, and my refrigerator isn't running either, so I don't need to go catch it."

"What are you talking about, Eli?"

"What are *you* talking about, Tan? I thought we were playing telephone games like seven-year-olds."

"Oh, yeah. No. I just had a weird summons to appear from some weirdo who calls himself Colonel and who wants me to meet him at the ass crack of dawn to go fishing in an area that's like two and a half hours away. His assistant bossed poor old Opal around so much, I was afraid she was going to break down in tears."

Eli's voice lowered to a whisper as he asked, "You're contemplating 'going fishing' with another man? Tanner!" Then he burst out laughing.

"Ha-ha. I'd never do *that*. But seriously, Eli, see if you can figure out who this guy is. Maybe it's legitimate. I don't want to piss off anyone at this stage, even though I told Opal to decline the invitation for me. If the guy wants to meet about my campaign, he can do it at a more convenient time." Tanner stared out the window and watched a group of kids walking down the sidewalk. He wondered idly if one of them would ever want his job someday.

"Don't worry, Tan. I'll look into it and let you know as soon as I can." There was a little pause and he added, "Zoë just got back from her errand. Would you like us to bring you some lunch?"

"Thanks, Eli. You're the best. I'll see you when you get here. Anything would be fine for lunch." After disconnecting the call, Tanner called his mother.

"Tanner! Nice to hear from you, son. Can you and Zoë come over for dinner soon?" Mrs. Lassiter was always up for a family dinner, especially now that Zoë was part of the family.

"Hi, Mama. We'll have to talk about it. Thanks. You know things are really crazy right now, and the town is planning the Honeybee Festival along with all of my campaigning, so..." he trailed off hoping she'd get the picture. When all she did was huff at him, he barged on, "Mama, have you ever heard of some character in Kentucky who calls himself Colonel? Not Sanders. I don't know his last name actually."

She laughed and answered, "I guess he was all in the news while you and Eli were off at Princeton. He's been pretty quiet about his business since then, but he's sort of a big deal in chicken farming. He's also as eccentric as they come and as rich as Croesus."

"Huh. Interesting. Hang on, Mama, just a sec. Actually, I'll have to call you back later. Bye now." He hung up and headed out to Opal's desk where she looked perplexed.

"Any luck with the meeting?" he asked as she looked at him with a frown.

"No," she said with pursed lips. "I was sent to voicemail, and the recording said the box was full, so I couldn't even leave a message."

"Well, they sent an email, can you just email them back?"

She frowned again and showed him the return address was one that said DoNotReply@TheColonel.com.

"Excuse me, Opal. I need to call my mama back." He started to head back to his office and abruptly turned back around. "Or maybe you know. She said this colonel character was in the news a lot maybe ten or so years ago? He's some kind of chicken farmer who has more money than sense?"

The lights went on in Opal's eyes. "Oh, yes! How could I forget that? I must be I' Oldtimer's," she laughed self-consciously. "He got himself embroiled in chicken wars when he tried to sell his chickens under the name 'Colonel's Chicken.' That didn't go over very well, and he was given a cease and desist order, so he tried to sue for the right and got handed his butt in a basket." Opal blushed, "Excuse my language, Mayor Lassiter."

"It's fine, Opal. So, what else can you remember about him?"

She scrunched up her face in thought and chewed her lip. "Hmm. He has a wife who's a lot younger'n he is. Quite a looker, if I remember." Tanner chuckled at that, and she went on, "He seemed like a big bag of wind when he was interviewed on the news."

"So, it doesn't sound like he's too dangerous—just a weirdo?"

"I wouldn't be able to comment on that with any confidence. He seems like a wily one. Why don't you go ahead and meet with him and take Mr. Whittaker with you? There's always safety in numbers, and if this really is about your campaign, your campaign manager ought to be in on the meeting. If the old windbag doesn't like it, he can just lump it!" Her cheeks went pink with her outburst.

Eli and Zoë waltzed in carrying fragrant bags of food. The aroma of French fries filled the office. "Lunch is served," Eli announced. "We brought you a big juicy cheeseburger too, Opal. We left the onions off in case you're expecting to get any action later."

He winked at her and her blush increased as she giggled. "Oh, you go on, Mr. Whittaker! My Alfred will be much appreciative, I'm sure. Mrs. Lassiter, you're looking as pretty as a picture today, I must say. Thank y'all for lunch."

So, over burgers, Opal and Tanner filled them in on the summons to appear and Opal's opinions. They all agreed it was a fine idea, and Eli announced, "I haven't been fishing in a while. I've missed it."

Tanner had to suppress a snort. "We'll need new Kentucky fishing licenses. Good thing I know people in high places who can get us some quickly. I just hope he doesn't have a little two-seater boat or something."

Smiling contentedly, Eli responded, "If he does, we'll just rent a bigger one for the day. And—we'll take the helicopter and get there in an hour or less. This is going to be fun, Tan, no matter what the old coot turns out to be like."

Later that evening when they all got home, Caro showed up with the research she'd done on this Colonel idiot. Over dinner, she shared her information with them.

Looking at her notes, Caro recited, "He's 74 years old, originally a native of Arkansas, but moved to Kentucky twenty years ago. He has an ex-wife and three kids who refuse to have anything to do with him, and he's currently married to his niece."

Squinching up her face, Zoë squeaked, "Ew! Isn't that illegal?"

"It is, so they had to go to Argentina to do the deed. It's legal in some countries," Caro explained. "Apparently, they haven't been interested in procreating, so that's good. A niece and uncle union, also called and avunculate marriage, is considered a much closer relationship genetically than first cousins marrying." She leveled them with a look. "You can imagine why his kids aren't too happy to be around him."

"So, what's this character's name? And why does he call himself Colonel?" Tanner asked.

Chuckling, Caro replied, "His given name is Arvol Silas Smelzer. Now there's a guy who'd love to monogram everything, wouldn't you say?" She ended her question with a snort. "His family started calling him Colonel as a joke when he was a little boy. He liked to play with his toy soldiers, and—the details are fuzzy here—his favorite was some colonel he aspired to be or something. The nickname apparently stuck."

"Wow," breathed Eli. "Nice work, Caro. So, do you know what floats his boat these days?"

"Well, sometime in his twenties he married and they had children spread out over about ten years. Years later, when he started cheating on his wife with his sister's sixteen-year-old daughter, his wife moved out, taking the kids. Sometime after that, he relocated to Kentucky. He comes from old family money, but he's a cutthroat businessman. His dealings have run the gamut from chicken farms, to casinos, fast food franchises—you name it. And you won't be surprised to hear that he's considered a strong political supporter when he sees someone he wants to back. He's a power broker to be reckoned with, but he can't seem to stick to one thing for very long. He's flighty and fickle and considered a very dangerous enemy to have."

Looking thoughtful and a little perturbed, Tanner mused, "Interesting. And he wants to meet with me? Does this mean he thinks I have a good chance of winning the election or that I'm young and moldable?"

Caro shrugged. "That's anyone's guess at this point. I guess you'll have to go fishing with him and see for yourself. If nothing else, you'll get some sun and maybe catch a trout or two." She took a drink and continued, "Worst case scenario, he ruins your political career somehow."

Eli chimed in, "That definitely would be the worst. Holy crap, what a strange man."

"Mama and Opal both said he was pretty odd back when he was in the news with his failed chicken marketing plan," Tanner said.

Caro continued, "Since that fiasco, he's apparently tried to stay completely out of the news. He's almost a recluse, so that explains the summons to appear on his terms and his lack of communication. I get the sense from the articles about him I dredged up that he's a little like Howard Hughes in that way, only with a lot less charm."

"Yeesh," exclaimed Zoë. "I wonder what he's going to try to get you to do for him, Tanner, in exchange for his support."

"Heaven only knows," Caro sighed as Tanner stared uncomfortably at his wife.

Chapter Twenty-Nine

Saturday was going to be a gorgeous sunny day. Both men silently donned tees and cargo shorts and grabbed their favorite fishing hats. They left Zoë sleeping in the middle of the big bed, each kissing a patch of her bare skin as they took off. Their driver took them to the parking lot in town where the helicopter sat waiting for them.

When they touched down about an hour later in the marina parking lot that had been magically cordoned off for their arrival, they both hopped off the helicopter looking fresh and ready to greet the day.

A short, grizzled old man in baggy pants and a floppy hat stood on the dock glowering at them as they wandered toward him laughing and chatting quietly. Eli looked beyond the man and took in the sight of—as he'd expected—an attractive yet minimal fourteen-foot fishing boat equipped with only two passenger seats and was piloted by the guide sitting by the rear motor. The old man wore a watch that cost as much as some houses, so this had to be Colonel.

"Good morning, Mr. Smelzer," Eli happily crowed as he stepped in front of Tanner. "I'm Elison Whittaker, and this is Mayor Lassiter. It looks like a fine day for fishing, don't you agree?" He stuck out his hand cordially.

Glaring, Smelzer shook with an iron grip that Eli returned twofold, noticing the tiniest grimace from the greasy old coot. Then Tanner apparently did the same thing as he explained,

"Mr. Whittaker is my campaign manager, so I thought it would be appropriate for him to sit in on this meeting. He's also a very talented fisherman." He stole a glance at Eli who gave the tiniest wink. Really—it could have just been something in his eye.

"There's only room for two and you can call me Colonel." Smelzer huffed unwelcomingly.

With a big smile, Eli chimed in cheerfully, "No problem at all, Mr. Smelzer. Here's our boat now. We'll have our man load anything you need onto it right away, and I think the chef ought to have breakfast ready for us any moment now. I know I'm starved. How about you, Mayor Lassiter?" They all three watched as a gorgeous cabin cruiser pulled into the slip next to the small fishing boat—completely dwarfing it. It had a large cabin with a canopied area behind it that had a table and chairs set up for a meal. There were four comfortable looking, sparkling white fishing chairs on the rear deck, and it gleamed from stem to stern with modern, sleek appointments. There was a crewman who was neither cooking nor piloting the boat—a burly guy who doubled as a bodyguard from Eli's employ. As soon as the guide maneuvered the boat into position, this temporary deckhand hopped off to secure it in place with sturdy dock lines.

Smelzer turned and narrowed his eyes menacingly at Eli. Then he stalked off to speak to his own fishing guide. After a few words, the old man's guide unloaded a cooler, tackle box, and a fishing pole onto the dock. Then Smelzer marched back and announced, "You won't try to get on my bad side if you know what's good for you, boy."

Eli smiled benignly at Smelzer and gave a small nod to the crewman who went to retrieve the old man's paraphernalia. They all climbed aboard and were immediately and politely asked to produce their fishing licenses to the guide.

"Let's get comfortable here and eat before we take off," Eli commanded as he escorted Tanner and Smelzer to the breakfast table. Fresh coffee and juice were already at each place, and immediately a uniformed chef served plates of omelets and fresh fruit in front of them. "Thank you, Oscar," Eli said to the chef. "Are these your famous herb and truffle omelets?"

"Yes sir, Mr. Whittaker. Just as you ordered. The ham is imported Black Forest, and the fruit and herbs are all locally produced. The truffles are, of course, from France. Enjoy, gentlemen, and let me know if you need anything else. I'll be right back with some fresh bakery items as well."

Tucking into their delicious breakfast, Eli and Tanner stayed quiet as they'd agreed to previously. They didn't want to seem aggressive, inquisitive, or even the least bit interested in what the old coot wanted to say. He could say it or not.

After an uncomfortable silence, however, Tanner's sense of southern manners kicked in and he tried to make things at least cordial. "So, Mr. Smelzer..."

"Colonel!" he interrupted.

"Yes, of course," Tanner said smoothly. "What kind of fishing do you like to do here? Rainbow? Catfish? Some of the bigger species? I've heard the rainbow trout here are terrific, and my wife is anxious for me to bag a few to bring home today."

"Hmmph," was his only reply. "Pass the pepper." He reached toward Tanner with a bony hand that looked ominously like it wanted to grab something and hang onto it long enough to squeeze the life out.

Eli, who'd finished most of his breakfast already, stood and said, "If you'll excuse me a moment, I'll just have a word with the guide. I'm sure he'd like to get underway. I'll let him know you're hoping for rainbow trout, Mayor Lassiter, and he'll know where to take us."

As soon as Eli was out of earshot, Smelzer sneered, "Nice little show you boys have going on here. You might want to consider, however, that you're going to need *local* support for your campaign, *Mayor* Lassiter." He said "mayor" like an epithet.

Smiling kindly, Tanner said in a soothing voice, "I'm fully aware of the need for Kentucky support, Mr. Smelzer. I'm sure you realize why we felt the desire to roll out the red carpet for you. Nothing is too good for my loyal supporters."

Smelzer squinted his eyes in doubt. Clearly, he'd believed they were trying to one-up him to show how *little* they needed his support. "I'm not one of your supporters *yet,* sonny boy. Politics is an interesting business..."

"I'm well aware," chuckled Tanner.

"...that relies on a healthy give and take of—let's call them favors," Smelzer continued in an oily voice. "I give you support and my public endorsement, and you agree to do something for me." He leveled a glare at Tanner. "I can make you or break you in this election, Lassiter. Mark my words."

Just then, Eli returned. He sat down and swallowed the last of his fresh orange juice. Smiling, he announced, "We're in great luck. The guide assures me the best place for rainbow trout is just about a mile that direction." He waved a hand upriver. "We'll be fishing in just moments." Then he grabbed what was left of his blueberry muffin and popped that into his mouth with a grin.

Sighing contentedly as the chef approached them to clear the table, Tanner said, "The breakfast was delicious, Oscar. Thank you for making it such a special treat. I grew up fishing with my daddy, and we never had anything but squashed peanut butter sandwiches and warm Cokes, so this was spectacular."

Oscar smiled broadly and answered, "Happy to oblige, sir. I'll also provide a variety of cold beverages and snacks throughout the day for you."

"Did you fix everything here onboard?" Tanner asked.

Oscar answered politely, "No sir. Just the omelets. The rest was prepared and brought on board. The galley is minimal, but nice. I'll have no trouble fixing your fish for lunch when you'd like it, but just in case the fishing isn't what you'd hoped, we have backup sandwiches as well."

Nodding and smiling, Tanner then turned to Eli and continued, "Mr. Smelzer here was just explaining to me how politics works. Apparently, he's a proponent of the 'you scratch my back, I'll scratch yours' approach. He has yet to say where it itches, however."

Smelzer scowled at them.

For the next few hours, nothing at all was discussed beyond the size of the fish they caught and what seemed to be attracting the fish to their lines. Tanner caught a beautiful twenty-one-inch rainbow and then three that were about fourteen inches. Oscar took those to prepare for their lunches. The large one was put on ice to take home. Eli rapidly landed his limit of five trout all under fifteen inches and decided to change it up for the rest of the day and do some catch and release. He pulled out a fly reel and tried that a few times, laughing that he'd never catch on to that technique. Deciding it was too much work, he finally sat back in the shade and relative coolness of the canopy and watched the beautiful day go by as he thought about how happy he was with Tanner and Zoë.

The whole time they fished, the bodyguard scanned their surroundings with an eagle eye and helped handle the fish for them once they were caught. He was like an efficient, mostly silent giant who took care of whatever needed doing.

Tanner and Eli had to point out to Smelzer that two of the fish he caught could earn him a big fine if he didn't release them. He grumbled a lot about the goodie-two-shoes assholes at the Fish and Wildlife Department and tossed back the fish with some colorful swear words.

Eli would have bet good money that Smelzer would have kept the illegally-sized fish had they not been there to insist that he release them. Everything about the old man made his skin crawl.

After a delicious lunch of fresh-cooked trout, Eli and Tanner were tired and ready to call it quits. They'd soaked in more sun than was necessary and wanted to spend what was left of the day with Zoë. Eli suggested, "A cold beer sounds good while we head back. Anyone else want me to grab one for you?" He headed toward the refrigerator in the covered area where they'd been eating.

But he stopped before opening it when Smelzer suddenly demanded, "You boys bourbon drinkers?"

Laughing, Tanner answered, "Of course. I grew up in Kentucky. Eli's become a convert."

"Then forget the lame-ass beer and let's have a real drink." Smelzer headed to his previously unopened cooler. The bodyguard watched the man closely as Smelzer reached inside. There seemed to be a bottle nestled among a bunch of peanut butter sandwiches in plastic bags and a few apples. Satisfied that the old guy wasn't producing a weapon, the bodyguard silently stepped back.

"Get me some glasses, and you'll both experience something new and special," he ordered in a crabby voice. The bodyguard quickly placed three glasses on the table, and Smelzer ignored the man. He brandished a bottle of something that was unfamiliar to Eli and Tanner.

After pouring three shots of an amber liquor into the glasses, Smelzer handed one to Eli and one to Tanner. He held his own aloft and cackled, "Here's mud in your eye!" and he downed his own in one gulp.

Frowning, Tanner sniffed at his own glass, and Eli did the same. Then both men took a tentative sip and grimaced.

"What is this?" asked Tanner. "It doesn't taste much like bourbon to me."

"More like rot gut," mumbled Eli as he stared questioningly at Tanner. He sniffed the glass again with a quizzical scowl.

Undaunted, Smelzer broke out into the first smile they'd seen from him all day. It looked like a lecherous grin and was terribly off-putting. "This here's my pet project, boys!" He poured another glass for himself as he smacked his lips eagerly. "It's gluten-free, low-calorie bourbon. If I can market it that way, I'll make a killing. How do you like that?"

Tanner took his seat again next to Eli at the table and said, "Have a seat, Mr. Smelzer." Smelzer sat, and his expression lost all of its former happiness. He was back to surly in an instant, but Tanner explained to him, "First of all, I've toured enough of Kentucky's fine distilleries to know that bourbon is already gluten-free because of the distillation process of the corn that's used in its production. And second of all, why would anyone care if it has fewer calories?"

Snorting as if Tanner were an imbecile, Smelzer huffed, "Health, sonny boy. Some people want a drink that won't make 'em fat. They wanna think they're drinkin' the *state beverage*, but there hasn't been a bourbon before mine that fits this niche. I could corner the market on health-conscious, weight-conscious drinkers with this and make a mint! I got the idea when my wife stopped drinkin' because of the extra calories. Named it after her too." He proudly showed them the bottle that had a curvaceous woman on the label with the name Payslee Premium Bourbon just below her tits. "She loves *this* stuff."

Eli squinted at him and asked, "Are you even able to get this stuff licensed? Is it really bourbon? I think it tastes like shit."

"You watch your mouth, smartass," Smelzer growled at Eli. "Of course, it's licensed." Turning to Tanner, he explained,

"This is where you and your truffle-eatin' *pretty boy* here come in handy, though." He had a nasty gleam in his eye that sent shivers down Eli's spine. "You might want to call off your goon here for a minute unless you want him to get an earful of some shit you don't want made public."

Eli instructed his guard to step to the bow of the boat where he and the guide were out of earshot but could still see them.

As the big guy ambled away, Smelzer turned his beady eyes on Tanner and asked, "You ever hear the one about the young man who goes into a bar and asks for five shots of bourbon?" He didn't wait for a reply before he went on with the rest of his story. "The bartender asks, 'Why so many shots, son?' So, the guy tells him, 'I'm celebratin' my first blowjob.' Then the bartender says, 'Congratulations. How was it?' The young guy answers, 'Pretty good, but now I need to get the taste outta my mouth.'" Smelzer cackled wildly at his stupid joke as Eli and Tanner sat stone-faced. "Get it?" He glared at them. "Course you do."

The chills running down Eli's spine at this point turned into a full-on glacier. He was afraid to even glance at Tanner who hadn't said a thing.

Smelzer leaned forward with a greedy look. "See, boys, here's the thing. I understand that you," he looked at Tanner, "have an uncle who's a member of the Kentucky Distillers' Association—and," he addressed Eli, "your daddy has a shit ton of money. With your wealth and connections, we can get this product steamrolled into action, and I can make a fortune." He looked back at Tanner with a malevolent took. "You need to figger out how to deal with the Distillers' Association so they'll give me a membership. You get that done, and I won't show your pretty little wife a camera full of pictures I have locked in my safe."

"What are you talking about?" asked Tanner with a furrowed brow.

Squinting malevolently, Smelzer explained, "A few years back, you started showing up everywhere in the press. It didn't take a genius to understand it meant you had political ambitions beyond that dumpy little Hillbilly Holler you call a town. So, I watched and I listened and discovered I was right. I also had a tail put on you immediately. Right away, you took off for a pretty remote area to take your nasty little trip, but the good thing about that was that you felt safe in that cabin and never closed any curtains. I got some pretty fuckin' dirty photos of you two. They're all still on the camera, and they ain't been released anywhere… yet. Do as I say, and you'll get the camera and the governorship handed to you. Defy me, and yer pretty wife may just have a change of heart towards her husband. Get it?"

Eli fumed internally. *As if Zoë would care!* Still, the prospect of those photos getting out was awful, and he didn't trust Smelzer at all.

"We can always claim the photos are doctored," mused Tanner. Eli noticed Tanner's face had lost a lot of color.

Smelzer's attention turned quickly to Tanner. "I hear your pretty little wifey is a smart gal. You really think she'd buy that?"

Tanner buried his face in his hands and mumbled, "No. Not really. I guess you have us over a barrel, Mr. Smelzer… Colonel."

"Now that's more like it, sonny boy. Yer learnin'—finally." He smiled his devilish leer at them and said in a nasal tone, "So here's what you need to do." He looked to see that he had their attention. "I want to be listed as a Heritage Distiller on the Kentucky Bourbon Trail. All of the visitors who travel through the state on the tasting tour can get their passports stamped at *my* distillery too, and I can add that prestigious classification to the labels on my bottles. I'll be happy to furnish free samples of this wonderful bourbon, and I'll be providing a public service by giving them a low-cal, gluten-free beverage."

Tanner chewed on the inside of his cheek and nodded slowly. "I guess I'll be having a chat with my uncle soon. But I have to ask, why haven't you just approached the board members yourself?"

"I've tried, sonny boy. They act like my money ain't good enough for 'em. But we all know the power of a family connection, so I expect you to grease the wheels for me. You do, and you get the camera and my endorsement. You don't, and you can kiss your political aspirations goodbye. Those photos will spread like wildfire after your wife sees 'em. You'll be out a wife *and* a career." Smelzer gave a satisfied cackle that made Eli and Tanner's skin crawl.

As they all disembarked back at the marina, Smelzer reached into his pocket and produced a business card. "This here's my private number. I expect to hear some great news from you—and soon," he ordered as he handed it to Tanner. Without a word of thanks or a goodbye, he headed toward the parking lot.

"Charming man," Eli whispered as they watched him stomp away. Then he burst out laughing and said, "At least he thinks I'm pretty."

Chuckling, Tanner gave Eli an affectionate slap on the back.

About a minute later, a uniformed driver came to retrieve all of Smelzer's equipment and his fish.

Chapter Thirty

The first thing Eli did when they got home was arrange to have his detective track down the PI who'd followed them and shot the photos. He wanted to verify that Smelzer knew what he was talking about and he needed to shut down any possible leaks. The next thing he did was to sit down with Tanner and Zoë for a chat.

"If someone brings you a package or an envelope of any kind, do *not* open it around anyone else," he ordered Zoë. "Tanner is being blackmailed by a nasty old codger who says he has photos of the two of us that will ruin your marriage." He looked at Tanner then and said, "At least we know his game plan now anyway."

Zoë smiled sweetly and snorted delicately, "As if." Then she squirmed a little and added, "I wouldn't mind seeing those photos, though. Maybe y'all can reenact them for me tonight." She gave them both a sultry look. "I'm sorry he's trying to ruin you, though, Tanner. He sounds horrible."

***

Tanner spoke to the Kentucky Distillers' Association that was in charge of the Kentucky Bourbon Trail to find out their regulations. Tanner got one woman on the phone who was so chatty, he ventured a question as to whether she'd had any requests from a distillery called Payslee Premium Bourbon.

Laughing, she answered, "Oh my, yes. The owner has made himself something of a pest. I've tried to explain to him he needs to be established and have a minimum barrel count of over ten thousand barrels a year before he can apply to our Proof Distillery membership and a minimum of twenty-five thousand barrels a year for our Heritage Distillery membership. He can certainly apply for a Craft Distillery membership —once his barrel count reaches the minimum level, but he doesn't seem to want that level of prestige and thinks he can just buy his way into a position as a voting member of the board of directors. I don't think he realizes that our Heritage level members are the premier bourbon distillers in the entire world. He can't just bully his way in because he has money. Sorry, I think I've said too much. That was out of character for me, Mayor Lassiter. Please forgive my talkativeness. He's not a friend of yours, is he?"

"Not a problem, ma'am," Tanner assured her. "He's definitely no friend of mine. I just wondered how he's been doing with his request. He's trying to get me to grease the way for him, but I'm not sure that what he brews is worthy of your illustrious labeling."

"Well, that's not all, Mayor Lassiter," she said conspiratorially. "He needs to find another member distillery to sponsor his application before we'll consider it, and so far, he hasn't had any luck there either."

"I see," Tanner mused. "Well, I certainly thank you for your information. And I hope come November I can count on your support at the polls."

"Oh, most definitely," she answered with a smile in her voice. "I like what you stand for, and I hope you win. It was a pleasure talking with you. Give my best to that pretty wife of yours. I hope I can meet you both someday."

Tanner's next call was to his uncle. Fred Lassiter was actually Tanner's great-uncle, and they didn't know each other particularly well because Fred's business and home were clear across the state, but Tanner thought the man might be open to speaking to him seeing that they *were* related and Tanner *was* running for governor.

Tanner was mistaken.

Uncle Fred was not the least excited about Tanner's candidacy because he was running for the wrong party, and as soon as Tanner mentioned Arvol Smelzer, his uncle nearly hung up on him. Instead, he gave Tanner an earful. "Listen, Tanner, don't you go getting yourself mixed up with the likes of that arrogant, lying cheater. If you get mixed up with him, you'll be selling your soul to the devil."

Soothingly, Tanner explained, "Yes, Uncle Fred, I understand that. I'm not trying to help the man, just make him think I am. He's... well... blackmailing me, and I'd like to turn the tables on him."

"Oh! Well, that's a different barrel of whiskey, son," Fred laughed softly. "I'm sorry you can't see it in your heart to run on the correct party's ticket, but blood is thicker than water, so what can I do to help?"

They had a brief discussion after which they both disconnected, satisfied.

***

Eli's office at the campaign headquarters began receiving calls from people offering provisional support for Tanner's campaign in the form of large donations and huge blocks of confirmed voters, but each promise hinged on whether or not they got approval from Colonel.

All the while, his PI tried and tried to track down anyone who'd been employed by Smelzer to tail Tanner and him. Each time the PI reported back to Eli, it was with no positive results. It was as if the man had vanished.

Tanner got a phone call on his cell one day in late September. It was from an unknown number, so he let it go to voice mail. His curiosity got the better of him before he deleted the message, so he was treated to a familiar nasally voice commanding him, "Tick tock, cocksucker. I ain't gettin' any younger. Let's see some results, or you'll be sorry!" Tanner saved the message.

Chapter Thirty-One

On a rainy afternoon in October, Tanner and Eli's driver pulled up to the front of Tanner's office. They'd been at a meeting with an important Kentucky corn growers' association listening to the farmers' ideas, and things had gone well, Tanner thought. He and Eli were all smiles until they realized there was a strange man standing outside of Tanner's office in the rain. He wore a raincoat and a brimmed hat that was pulled way down so that they couldn't see his face at all. Rather than exiting the car, Tanner ordered the driver to go around the block and phoned Opal.

"Do you know anything about the guy getting himself soaked out front?" he asked her.

Sighing, Opal explained, "He's looking for you. Says he has to tell you something important—something private. I told him you'd be a while, so he left and came back a couple of minutes ago."

"Huh," Tanner mused. "You didn't tell him to get inside out of the rain?"

"I tried to. Do you want me to call the sheriff?"

"Nah, thanks Opal. We'll have the bodyguard check him out and get him somewhere to dry off. Now I'm curious." Tanner hung up and explained the situation to Eli, telling the driver to head back.

They again pulled up to the front of the building and Tanner rolled down the window.

Seeing the mayor's face, the man hurried toward the car. His progress was hampered immediately, when Tanner's bodyguard intercepted him. After a brisk and thorough frisking, the guard stepped back with a nod.

"Sorry about that, sir," began Tanner in a soothing voice. "Can't be too careful. I understand you'd like a word with me?"

"Yes sir, Mayor Lassiter." Leaning down for a better look into the car, the man appeared to be bolstered by something as he went on, "I see you have Mr. Whittaker with you too, and I'd very much like to speak to both of you." He looked around and added quickly, "Privately."

"Alright then, let's all head into my office, shall we?" Tanner asked as he opened the door to step out.

"Uh, how about we don't go in there? I don't want your assistant to hear this. Is the limo private?" Then the man closed his eyes briefly and shook his head. "I'm sorry, my name is Doug Freeman and I am employed by a man who calls himself Colonel." Doug was a nondescript, middle-aged white guy. Everything about him was so painfully average, he probably never got a second look from a single soul. He was the personification of beige.

Tanner opened the door, let Doug into the car, and instructed the driver to take them home. He didn't want the risk of anyone hearing this conversation. When Doug opened his mouth to speak, Tanner silenced him saying, "Wait just a few minutes, please, Mr. Freeman."

As soon as they got to the mayor's residence, they ushered Doug in, divested him of his dripping raincoat, hat, and soaked shoes, and Eli went to get the man a dry towel for his face while Tanner made him a hot coffee.

When they were finally comfortably seated around the kitchen table, Doug began his story.

"First of all, I feel I owe you both an enormous apology for invading your personal lives." Neither Tanner nor Eli responded to that, so he continued. "For several years I've worked as a private investigator, and, a few years ago, I was hired for a lucrative job by Colonel. I'd never met him before, and everything about the man rubbed me wrong, but my wife was ill and we have four kids." He took a fortifying drink from his coffee. "He paid me to tail you, Mayor Lassiter, so I did. I am extremely good at my job, if I do say so." For the first time, the man seemed to be growing a backbone, and the transformation was fascinating. His eyes lit up, his posture straightened, and he suddenly looked in charge—handsome even. "I took a collection of photos of the two of you on a fishing trip you took together and gave the camera with the photos inside to Colonel in exchange for enough money to put a huge dent in my financial troubles."

Eli's eyes became angry slits as a vein popped in his forehead.

Tanner's jaw clenched and his eyes flashed with irritation. He was sure they'd been so careful, but obviously not careful enough.

Doug hastened to add, "I'm terribly sorry for invading your lives." He raised two hands in a gentle protesting gesture. "Let me explain before you get angry." He looked between their annoyed faces. "I've done my share of taking photos of cheating spouses and dirty business partners, but when I saw the two of you together, I saw nothing wrong. I saw two attractive young men who apparently had a serious relationship. I found no evidence with my research that either of you were cheating on anyone, so I came to the conclusion that Colonel wanted the information for some kind of blackmail. I have since learned about his reputation as a political power broker, and I wanted nothing to do with his dirty deals. That didn't mean I could turn down the paycheck, however. Our eldest daughter was just finishing college and medical bills were piling up. It was a hard time for us." He rubbed his face and swallowed the rest of his coffee.

"More coffee?" asked Tanner. He still hadn't changed expressions much.

Eli hadn't moved an inch.

"No, thanks, I'm good now. That helped warm me up though." Doug gave a small smile. "Then I began to hear the rumors and rumblings about your bid for the governor's race, and I knew for sure, this was Colonel's way to manipulate. It made me ill."

Eli finally exploded. He stood and towered over Doug, shaking with fury. "Did you have fun watching, you sick fuck? Did you get your jollies seeing the two queers *do it?*"

"Please, Mr. Whittaker, hear me out." Doug didn't cower away from Eli's outburst, though many a man would have. "Shortly after I turned over the camera and memory chip, our daughter announced she planned to marry her college roommate, and I realized how horrible I'd feel if someone tried to exploit her sexuality for their own gain."

Eli sat down. He didn't stop glaring yet, though.

"I admit, I did see things I should not have, but I was so disgusted with Colonel... ugh... Whatsisname..."

"We call him Smelzer. That's his last name," Tanner interjected.

"Thank you. I hate giving that man any type of honorific that he obviously doesn't deserve." Doug took a deep, cleansing breath. "As I said, I gave the photos and the camera to Smelzer. You have my solemn word that not a trace of those images exists anywhere else. I watched him place the camera in his safe myself."

"That's a little bit of a relief, at least, but I hope," deadpanned Tanner, "that you're going to start in on the *good news* you have for us anytime now."

"Well, I actually do have some great news," Doug said with a tentative smile. "Smelzer hired me to do more surveillance work for him."

Eli's eyes skewered Doug as he snapped, "What's so good about that? You planning to mess around with someone else's life for him?"

Doug ignored Eli's outburst, and his face relaxed into a wide grin as he explained, "I came up with a plan for getting the memory chip out of the camera and Smelzer never knew."

Eli and Tanner's jaws dropped.

Looking self-satisfied, Doug explained, "When Col... Smelzer bought the camera from me, I had to go buy a new one just like it, but the more recent model of lens on the new camera isn't as nice as the one on the original. I told Smelzer I needed to switch lenses or I couldn't do his job as well as he'd like."

"What does the lens have to do with the memory card in the camera?" asked Tanner.

"Nothing at all, but I was able to pull out the card without Smelzer seeing me do it." He looked from Tanner to Eli, grinning. "I'd been practicing sleight of hand!"

Eli still looked skeptical as he demanded, "What if Smelzer decides he wants to check the camera again after you messed with it?"

"He won't. First of all, he doesn't know the first thing about how to work a camera, and second, he saw the photos once and declared then that he never wanted to look at them again as long as he lives. He's a horrible homophobe and treated the whole thing like it was going to turn him gay or something just by looking. Believe me, he does not want to look at those images a second time."

Tanner had a worried look on his face when he asked, "When did you do this? Recently?"

"Yes. I did it this morning," Doug answered in a firm voice. "I've just been waiting for an opportunity. When I saw that you'd won the primary, I knew it was time." Doug looked seriously into Tanner's eyes and stated, "I want you to win this election, Mayor Lassiter. My entire family plans to vote for you. If something should happen and those photos ever leaked, it would kill me to know I'd done anything to ruin a good man's career. I wanted to get that chip from the camera, and I want you to know you are free and clear of a threat from Smelzer."

Squinting at him, Tanner said, "Thank you, Mr. Freeman..."

"Call me Doug, please."

"Thank you, Doug," Tanner began again, "for your support at the polls." He looked into Doug's eyes and asked, "But how did you know that Eli and I knew about the camera and the blackmail scheme?"

Doug gave a wide smile and a wink. "I told you, I'm *very* good at my job. And not all of the investigation I do is for pay. Anything you need to be scoped out—I get it done. No one is ever the wiser."

"Then why are you telling us all of this?" demanded Eli.

Letting out a long breath, Doug replied, "It's my way of apology. I could have just done it and left it alone, but I wanted to make sure both of you had peace of mind." Doug reached into his pocket, produced the memory card, and handed it to Tanner with a smile.

"Now what are you planning to do? Aren't you worried about Smelzer once he figures out what happened?"

With a broad smile, Doug answered, "My wife has family in Sydney. So, if you'd please have your driver take me back to my car, I have plans to catch a redeye tonight with my entire family. We're heading to Australia for an indeterminate length of time." He looked happy as he finished, "We're all ready for an adventure. Oh, and I assure you, we all mailed in our absentee ballots already. We all voted for you."

Later that evening when Zoë got home, she found her men sitting in front of the glowing fireplace with three glasses of wine on the coffee table. A digital camera sat next to the wine.

As soon as she saw her men, a broad smile lit up her face. "Let's see it!" she demanded with a grin.

The photos made things abundantly clear that it was Tanner and Eli, but Zoë announced with a small grimace, "Looking at these makes me feel too much like a peeping Tom. I much prefer the real thing where I can reach out and touch you." She scooted the camera away on the coffee table and took a sip of wine.

After a couple of minutes of reminiscing about the great fish they'd caught on that trip, Tanner took the memory chip out of the camera and tossed it into the fireplace. They watched with satisfaction as it melted away to nothing.

"Are you completely sure this will get rid of Smelzer and his conniving?" Zoë asked nervously.

Eli grinned and Tanner chuckled, "Don't worry. We have more ideas on how to deal with that old buzzard."

Chapter Thirty-Two

Tanner's Uncle Fred Lassiter placed a call to Smelzer. "I have some great news for you," he announced magnanimously —and quickly. "We're going to be sending a photographer and reporter over to your distillery to record me discussing sponsorship consideration for your application to the KDA. This doesn't happen very often, so you ought to be very proud. Very proud, indeed! Congratulations."

Smelzer's snarly voice sounded even worse than usual when he grumbled, "It's about time."

Fred wondered if the man's parents had ever tried to instill *any* manners in him when he'd been a kid. He also wondered whether Smelzer caught onto his ambiguous wording. Probably not—the guy was such an egomaniac he would hear what he wanted to hear... hopefully.

Still grumbling, Smelzer demanded, "How long does the application process take once you've sponsored me? I don't want to wait for all eternity, ya know?"

"Well," Fred hedged, "these things happen in all good time. We'll do our very best to streamline the process for you to get the paperwork completed. I understand from my nephew that your product fills a particular niche, so that's certainly in your favor. He made an extremely strong case for your bourbon and sang your praises to the moon, so I for one am quite anxious to try it." *Lies.* Fred wondered if his nose was growing.

"Hmmph. Yeah," Smelzer grunted. "When is this supposed to happen?"

Fred took a deep breath and mentally crossed his fingers for the new lie he was about to tell. "I'm going to be out of the state for a while, so the first we can do this is the fifth of November."

"Well, that's *after* the damned election!" spluttered Smelzer.

"Yes, it is," answered Fred smoothly. "What of it? Whoever becomes the new president has no bearing on your application, does it? Am I missing something?" He had to stifle a laugh—the old coot was so transparent.

"Nah. I guess not," Smelzer backtracked. "Why can't y'all get over here today and take care of it?"

"Oh, I'm terribly sorry. I can't get away. Business matters, family matters... you know. That's just out of the realm of possibility. But I will see you on November fifth. We'd like to meet in your tasting room, so you'll want to have it photo-ready. I trust that won't be an issue." He heard more grumbling and took that to be an assent, so he said, "We'll be there at one in the afternoon. Please accept my hearty congratulations, Colonel, and we'll see you soon. Bye."

***

Smelzer had no choice now. He had to tell his special voter blocs to support Lassiter. The timing rankled him, but he was so anxious to start making a shit ton of money with his new gluten-free, low-cal bourbon, he couldn't see straight. And the idea of having voting rights on the prestigious board of the Kentucky Distillers'—damn! He could lord it over anyone he wanted to with that kind of power.

After making the appropriate calls, he launched himself out from behind his desk and went in search of his wife. He figured he deserved at least a congratulatory blow-job.

"Payslee! Where're you at?" he bellowed through the halls of his mammoth house. "Payslee!" He stopped by the bathroom and grabbed a little blue pill, swallowed it down and went off in search of his wife again. "Hey baby! Daddy needs to celebrate!"

Chapter Thirty-Three

A couple of weeks before the election, the incumbent first lady of Kentucky called Zoë. "Mrs. Lassiter, I'd love to extend an invitation to you and your husband to come and tour the Governor's Mansion privately. It's open to the public for tours twice a week, but that tour only covers the public areas. We think you'll be interested to see the upper floors as well— the private residence part."

"Thank you," Zoë answered with a big smile. "That would be very generous of you. I'm sure Tanner would like to see it as much as I would. We both went on the public tour back when we were students, but it's been many years." Zoë thought fast and decided to ask, "Would you mind if Tanner's campaign manager accompanied us on the tour? I'm sure he'd be just as interested as we are, and I'd love to include him if that's alright." She'd rather die than make Eli feel less than part of their union, she and Tanner loved him so much.

"Oh, um, no, I don't mind. That would be just fine. Is he a fan of state history or architecture possibly?"

Smiling to herself, Zoë answered, "Indeed he is. Eli is *quite* a fan of history." She thought to herself with a suppressed giggle that just last night Eli had been regaling them with a hysterical *and* historical account of his first sexual experience. He'd had them both in stitches.

So, Zoë accessed Tanner's calendar and conferred with Eli, and the two ladies were able to set up a date. They decided a couple of days after the election would be best. The first lady laughed and added, "I'm pretty certain your husband is going to take this one hands down, but... it's true that you never know until it's over. I wish you and Mayor Lassiter the very best of luck."

Chapter Thirty-Four

Tanner looked exhausted to Zoë, but he and Eli were also both so charged up about the rapidly approaching election, it was hard for them to contain themselves. They hip-hopped and crisscrossed the state day after day. Speeches, rallies, talk shows, colleges—you name it, Tanner did it. Sometimes Zoë went along, and other times, she had her own engagements. She was rapidly becoming as beloved as her husband. As a couple, they delighted people with their brains, gentility, good looks, and their obvious empathy for everyone they spoke to. Pictures of them showed up everywhere.

And Eli was always in the background. He organized, planned, observed, and made sure every detail was met with precision. The three of them were an indomitable team.

Tanner's words were received with raucous approval, and his fans were legion. No one close to him wanted to make a prediction, however, because you just never knew. Older people responded well to him—despite his young age—because he made sense to them, and he was obviously brilliant. Young people responded well to Tanner because he seemed like a fresh new face with ideas they could live with. Minorities responded well to him because he made it clear from the outset that he supported their needs, and he did it without pandering and sounding insincere.

One condescending reporter from a shady magazine tried to stir up controversy by making a ridiculous case that Tanner had some problem with the LGBTQ community. Tanner angrily shot that down in a big, fat hurry, demonstrating to voters that he was passionate about the cause and displaying a new side to his personality. He figured anyone who really *did* have a problem with the LGBTQ folks were people who could just keep their stupid votes and opinions to themselves. He wanted nothing to do with them until they wised up and realized this was the twenty-first century. After the episode happened, however, he had a fit of conscience and sat down to discuss it with Zoë and Eli.

It had been a long, emotionally draining day, and they were just finishing up a late dinner when Tanner asked with a troubled look, "Do you both think I should come out publicly and admit I'm bi-sexual after all? Am I missing a great opportunity for honesty and clarity? Are we making a mistake keeping it private?"

Eli was first to answer, "After all the effort we've extended to keep things private, I'd hate to mess up just before the election, Tan."

Zoë seemed deep in thought as she mused, "Tanner, it's your decision ultimately, but if you do out yourself, it's going to go way beyond just admitting your sexuality. Whom you sleep with is no one's business but ours, really, but it won't take long before people question your relationships and start snooping. Where the three of us are involved, a public acknowledgment would put us all in a never-ending fishbowl. You might still get elected, and then it would turn your governorship into a sideshow. I'm not sure that's how you want to serve the greater good. You'd make some people happy, but in the long run, I'm afraid you'd lose credibility and we'd lose every shred of privacy."

Sighing, Tanner took her hand. "You're right, Zoë. I'm just tired of worrying whether someone like Smelzer is going to make this all blow up in our faces. I'm in no way ashamed of us, but I understand that we're still a little ahead of the class when it comes to polyamory in Kentucky." He looked at Eli and asked, "So, you think we should still just stay private? It doesn't bother you?"

"Zoë's right that coming out now would put us under a spotlight that would detract from all of the good you can do as governor. It does bother me, of course, but looking at the big picture... I think we have to keep things the way they are. I can just imagine the rude questions people would feel justified to ask any of us."

Zoë looked at Tanner then and asked, "Do you think this is a good time to discuss with Eli what we talked about?"

Eli blinked and jolted back a little. "What?" he asked at the same time that Tanner smiled at Zoë and said, "Yes, this is a good time."

Tanner was still holding Zoë's hand, so he reached out his other and took one of Eli's as Zoë did the same. When they were all joined as a unit, Zoë announced, "Tanner and I have talked about this and we wanted your opinion as well. I'm thinking about going off the pill." She smiled sweetly at Eli.

"Um... kaaay..." Eli drawled. "I guess this means it's back to condoms for me?"

Zoë kept smiling and Tanner squeezed Eli's hand. "Not unless you want to, Eli. That's not what we mean. If you're ready for it, we were trying to think of how we could make our commitment to you as permanent and enduring as Zoë's and my marriage. We could write up some legal documents—which we should probably still do, or we could have a moving little ceremony amongst the three of us where we pledge our troth to you... or something. But in the long run, we feel that if you or I were to impregnate Zoë, and we don't care or try to even figure out who the father is unless we have to for some dire medical reason—well, we're married to you. Making a family with you is forever. Are you ready for this? Ready to be a dad?"

Eli sat there in stunned silence and then a tear trickled down his face. He whispered, "Oh my God, you two. You're... wow."

Zoë stood and wrapped her arms around Eli from behind. She bent over him and kissed his face. "Say yes, Eli. Say you'll father babies with us. We both love you so much."

Letting out a long, shuddering breath, Eli said, "I never thought this could happen to me in a million years. I never thought I could love two people the way I love you both. Thank you." He looked between the two of them and gasped as they both dropped to a knee before him.

"Marry us, Eli," demanded Tanner.

"Marry us *our own way*," implored Zoë.

"Yes, of course," whispered Eli. "Of course." He wrapped his arms around both of them in a tight embrace.

Batting her eyelashes coquettishly, Zoë asked, "Anyone feel like practicing making babies?"

They spent the next couple of hours doing just that. They were a writhing, gasping, kissing, sucking mass of bodies that finally ended up with Zoë in the middle of two hard men who pounded her from front and back, almost dueling inside her with their steely erections. After an orgasm ripped through her, taking her voice with it for a moment, Zoë realized she was the only one who'd climaxed so far.

"Hold up, guys, for just a moment," she panted.

"Are you alright" Tanner demanded. "Were we too rough on you?"

Zoë laughed, "Of course I'm alright. You know I love it like this. I just think we need to switch this around a little and let Eli celebrate being the cream filling in this cookie for once. It's not every day you decide to get married. Can we do that for him?"

Eli let out a growly moan. Apparently, he was on board with that idea, and he was already balls-deep in her pussy. This meant that Tanner pulled carefully out of Zoë's ass, changed condoms and lubed up Eli's butt. When Tanner sunk into Eli from behind, Zoë watched with delight as Eli's eyes rolled back in pleasure. It took a second or two, but gradually the two men created a rhythm again.

"It's good, isn't it, Eli? Being totally surrounded by love?" she asked him in a whisper. "Feel how much we adore you." For good measure, she clamped her muscles down on Eli, making him shudder with a groan into her neck. She intoned softly to him, "Eli, we promise to love you and honor you forever."

In only a moment, Eli tensed all over and shoved hard and deeply into Zoë. He climaxed hollering, "I love you both!" just as Tanner shuddered behind him and came as he yelled, "This *is* forever!"

As they lay wrapped snuggly around each other basking in the afterglow of amazing sex and pure love, Zoë began to recite, "We take you, Eli, to be our husband, to have and to hold from this day forward, for better or worse, for richer or poorer, in sickness and in health, to love and to cherish, until we are parted by death. This is our solemn vow."

Tanner picked up where she left off and intoned, "We take you, Eli to be our faithful husband understanding that marriage is a lifelong union, and not to be entered into lightly. We expect to raise our children with you as an equal parent in all things. This is our solemn vow."

With tears tracking his cheeks, Eli sat up and looked at both of them. "I never expected to marry anyone, but I promise to be your husband and to love and honor both of you as long as I live. I'll father children with you and love them as much as I love my husband and my wife. This is my solemn vow."

***

A few days later, Zoë took her last pill and tossed out the empty pack. This was going to be a new chapter in their lives.

She hoped it wasn't too much for them to handle with the election now just a couple of days away.

Chapter Thirty-Five

The polls showed Tanner running neck and neck with his opponent Buckman, but polls had been known to be way off base in the past, so it was hard to know whether or not to believe in anything they saw on TV or read online.

Suddenly, on election eve, the TV was filled with brand new information that Terrence Buckman had taken a huge jump in the polls, and he was confirmed as a sixty-seven percent choice for winning. Tanner muted the TV and laughed, "Isn't it interesting that the news anchors are never compelled to produce any information about the source for their so-called polls? One guy could have polled his five buddies over beers during happy hour, and it's 'news.'"

An hour later, "Colonel" Smelzer appeared on the screen, looking his craggy best and answering an anchor's questions, so Tanner turned up the sound again. "This ought to be rich," he snorted.

"Mayor Lassiter has all the makings of a fine governor of this great commonwealth. I know he's young, but he has a fire in his belly and he's certainly my choice." It seemed that Smelzer was winding up to make some longwinded speech, but he was cut off and not seen again after that. There were a few other interviewees who supported Buckman, citing Tanner's youth as a deterrent in their thinking. They didn't have a single reason to support Buckman—just the one reason not to support Tanner.

"Don't those idiots realize I have more experience after all of these years as mayor than Buckman has? There's just no reasoning with closed-minded people," Tanner sighed for the hundredth time.

They surfed around to other channels and didn't find anyone else that was predicting Tanner's doom. Finally, they just turned off the TV and went to bed. It had been such a tiring several weeks, Tanner was ready for the election to be in the rear-view mirror, no matter what the result at this point.

The next morning, dressed in their finest and giddy with excitement, they took off by limousine to the county courthouse to cast their votes. As Tanner and Zoë exited the vehicle, flashes went off from all directions. Questions were lobbed their way, and everyone was in an animated, jovial mood.

Tanner took the opportunity to pause and make a statement to the press. He looked so handsome in his tailored blue suit and red tie Zoë felt like she would burst with pride for him. It was a chilly fall day, so she also wore a blue coat over her red and white dress. They looked like the ultimate political dream couple as they stood holding hands while Tanner calmly addressed the onlookers making polite jokes and thanking people for their support. He finished with a heartfelt promise to work hard for the citizens of his beloved Kentucky. The clip instantly went viral, and folks throughout the state fell in love with them all over again.

Eli had a very good feeling about this day and the probable outcome. He'd changed his legal residency to Kentucky months before so he could also vote for Tanner.

The day dragged on and on, however. No voting numbers were allowed to be aired, so they just had to wait it out until the polls began to close. The airways were simply filled with empty prognostications that no one paid the least bit of attention to.

Kentucky is in both the eastern and central time zones, and the part of the state where they lived began to register their numbers shortly after six o'clock. And wouldn't you just know that, as the earliest numbers were reported showing Tanner at eighty percent of the vote, the newscasters repeated over and over again, "It's too early to call."

Precinct after precinct reported their votes, and Tanner's numbers rarely dipped below seventy-nine percent. He topped out in his home precinct at a solid ninety-five, however. Still, until the larger metropolitan areas were counted, the news refused to budge and say anything other than, "Too early to call."

Lexington, then Bowling Green, and finally Louisville reported their numbers, and Tanner was such a runaway favorite, Buckman gave his concession speech: "Congratulations to a fine young man. I wish Governor Elect Lassiter all the best in his political pursuits." It wasn't the least bit moving or brilliant, but it got Buckman out of the spotlight and home for a drink as soon as he was done thanking his supporters. One got a distinct impression from the man that he was relieved. Being governor would have been an awful lot of work.

Tanner wondered aloud as he hugged Eli with a tight grip, "Do you think he just ran after losing a bet with his golf buddies or something?" They both cracked up.

And still, one television reporter was seen telling the public on live camera, "The governor's race is still too close to call." She got a stricken look as her face turned red and she held her hand to her earpiece. "Oh!" she exclaimed, "I'm told that Buckman had conceded the race. Congratulations to Governor Elect Lassiter." She shot someone a dirty look, and the camera cut to another scene.

Chaos reigned at campaign headquarters. Champagne flowed, music blared, smiles and hugs and supreme joy were everywhere.

Tanner's loyal supporters were losing their minds. Nothing —truly *nothing* this exciting had ever happened in this town. Their golden boy was headed to the governor's mansion! The sense of pride and overall excitement was so strong, there was even a small baby boom nine months later. Three of the babies were named Tanner, and one was named Zoë.

After hours and hours of speeches, thanks, hugs, and phone calls from friends and family who weren't in Honeybee Hollow, the three of them finally headed back to the mayor's residence. It had been Tanner's home for so long, he felt a little nostalgic suddenly. "I wonder if I ought to sell this place or just rent it out," he mused as they wandered down the hall to the bedroom. "Well, I don't have to decide tonight—that's for sure."

Since they all smelled pretty strongly of champagne, showers were in order. But by the time Tanner and Eli made it into the bed, Zoë was already passed out in the middle. It was nearly four-thirty in the morning.

"I think she has the right idea," sighed Eli. He kissed Tanner, climbed in next to Zoë and passed out as well.

Tanner had a little more trouble falling asleep. His mind was full of the events of the day. He'd received a congratulatory phone call from the White House, for heaven's sake! And soon he'd be inaugurated as *governor*. He had Zoë and he had Eli in his life forever. There just weren't any more blessings he could imagine for himself.

He was so wrong, though. Life always has more blessings in store.

Snuggling as close to Zoë as he could, he reached across her to snag a part of Eli and finally found sleep.

Chapter Thirty-Six

As scheduled, they took off to visit the governor's mansion two days later. Just as Zoë and Tanner remembered from their school days, the house was incredible. It was filled room by room with priceless antiques and artwork. Zoë cringed inside thinking of having a toddler running through a house like this. The upper floors, however, were a lot homier, and she felt a bit more like she could breathe easily when they toured through the vast living areas.

The first lady was all gracious smiles and encouraging words as she introduced everyone to the staff, and she kindly hosted a small lunch for them so they could also appreciate the quality of the chef's work. She seemed to beam with pride over everything, and there was an air of nostalgia about her that let you know immediately that her eight years as Kentucky's first lady had been the pinnacle of her life so far and she'd sorely miss it. She had a good thirty years on them age-wise.

After a couple of hours, they took their leave. All three of them had been cordial and receptive, but when they got into the limo, they all let loose spectacularly and simultaneously.

"No way in hell!" cried Tanner. "That place is not for us. We need to *do* something."

"Ugh," Zoë moaned. "I feel like I'd be a prisoner in the top tower of a castle just waiting to be let out. And that food! Gross. Who eats like that anyway?"

Laughing and holding his stomach, Eli promised, "Don't worry, you two. I've been suspecting your reactions and I have something to show you." He gave an address to the driver who took them not too far away.

"Not all governors live in the prescribed mansions," he explained. "In fact, you'd have to pay to live in it. The mansion can be staffed and kept for state functions, so you'll still be expected to host events there. Kentucky is especially known for special performances and affairs, but the content is completely up to you. You can hold rock concerts or dance performances, movie screenings—whatever suits you. Or nothing at all if you're shy—though that won't endear you to many of your supporters who'd love to be invited to some swanky events now and then." Just then, the limo pulled through an electronic gate in a tall brick wall and came to a stop in front of a beautiful property on the outskirts of Frankfort. "Take a look at this place. I bought it for you as a congratulatory gift." He looked between their astonished faces with a wink. "Just in case. If you don't like it, I'll just sell it again."

"Eli!" Zoë gasped. She jumped out and took in the sight of a huge house on a couple of tree-filled acres. There was a carriage house on one side that was larger than most regular houses, and the architecture of the place was stunning. It was a true southern mansion and there was a warm, inviting air about it. She couldn't believe how beautiful it was.

Clearing his throat, Tanner looked at Eli. "You're amazing. Just look at how excited she is here, and she hasn't even seen the inside yet. You knew, didn't you, Eli? That she'd need a real house and not some historical monument to live in." They watched as Zoë wandered through the property looking at flower beds and obviously imagining what they'd look like when the spring came. Her face glowed with joy. "I can't thank you enough, Eli." He leaned forward and whispered in Eli's ear, "I want to kiss you so badly right now." Pulling back, he locked eyes with Eli. They didn't always need words for what they needed to communicate.

"Well, let's see the indoors too, shall we?" Eli responded with a proud but shy smile. She strode to the front door and quickly opened it with a key.

Indoors was even better. Sunlight poured in, making everything gleam. It was colorful and warm, and even though the place was huge, it felt like a family home. Their home.

"Since I'm taking on the job as Chief of Staff, no one will bat an eye at me living in the carriage house." As Zoë and Tanner's heads whipped around to face him with incredulous looks, he laughed. "But I think we'll just let the public believe that. I've spoken to Chef Oscar about actually moving into it with his husband Dante. And..." he paused for drama, "Dante, as it turns out, has a very strong background and glowing references as a manny."

"Wonderful! You'll love Oscar's food, Zoë. I promise," Tanner declared with a wide grin.

"When can we move in? We kind of need furniture though..." Zoë asked as she gawked from room to room. "What's the master bedroom like?" Now and then she'd stop dead in her tracks and exclaim, "Look at this! Wow." She was currently surveying the enormous professional-grade kitchen with every appliance she'd ever dreamed of on shiny display.

Eli chuckled and put his arm around Zoë's waist. "I've had Caro working with a designer for a couple of weeks, and they have some plans for you to approve. Best case scenario would be in three weeks, if you'd like."

Zoë's chin dropped and she started to laugh. "No wonder Caro's been asking me so many oddball questions lately about favorite colors and what kind of sheets I like to sleep on. I just told her, 'clean ones.'" She looked lovingly at Tanner and Eli, "You guys, this is going to be amazing. Now let's see the bedroom!"

At the same time as they were all losing their minds over the exquisite house Eli had procured for them, in another part of the state Caro Whittaker was hard at work on a different project. She had made arrangements with Tanner's Uncle Fred Lassiter to pose as a news crew and meet with him at Smelzer's distillery. It was time to deal with that man once and for all.

Flanked by a sound engineer, cameraman, and a lighting guy, Caro exuded all of the right vibes as a self-important reporter as she and Uncle Fred followed Smelzer into his tasting room. Caro barked a few orders and kept an eye out for Smelzer and what he could see. The man was so full of himself he was basically frothing at the mouth as he poured generous glasses full of whatever the hell he was trying to foist off as low-cal, gluten-free bourbon. His wife Payslee seemed to flutter around him like a deranged moth. She bumped into Smelzer a few times with her enormous boobage, causing him to spill the liquor. Each time that happened, she let out a self-conscious giggle that had Smelzer glaring at her.

Finally, the lights were set, the mics were live, and drinks were handed out. Caro announced into her mic in front of the cameraman, "I'm here today with Fred Lassiter, a long-time member of the prestigious Kentucky Distillers' Association. He's here to discuss membership with Payslee Distillers." Looking at Smelzer she said, "Colonel, I understand this is a big day for you and something you've been working toward for a while now. Tell us a little about how your bourbon is going to offer people something new."

Puffing out his chest, Smelzer began a long-winded explanation about gluten-free and low calories. Payslee took a slosh of her drink and smacked her lips approvingly as her husband spoke. He didn't get very far into his diatribe, however, when the sounds of choking and retching came from Uncle Fred. The camera swung to Fred's red face.

"Jesus Christ, man! You call this shit *bourbon?*" he hollered. "What's the matter with you?"

Then, just to make things even more exciting, Payslee started screaming her stupid head off. She clutched her husband and thrust him in front of her as she shrieked, "Daddy! A rat! There's a rat in the food!" And sure enough, amidst the fruit, cheeses and fancy crackers, a big, healthy brown rat had taken up residence and was happily snacking away on the goodies set out for him. Two more of his buddies then hopped up onto the table to help out, and Payslee ran screeching from the tasting room.

Smelzer's eyes narrowed as he glared at Uncle Fred. "We don't have a fucking rat problem in this distillery. What's going on here?"

"Well, you also don't seem to have *bourbon* in this distillery if this is what you want us to promote for you," Fred said as he wiped his chin. "I suggest you abandon the project or bring someone in who knows what they're doing. This is an abomination!"

"I thought that sneaky little nephew of yours was making sure I was approved!" Smelzer shot back at him. "This was just a joke to him all along, wasn't it?" He turned to Caro and announced, "Would your TV station like a real scoop about our new pansy-ass governor? You know he's a flamin' *queer*? I have proof! All that posing with his nice little wife is nothing but a big fat lie. He's been boning that pretty boyfriend of his for years." With that, Smelzer ran out of the room, forgetting to close the door behind him.

One of the rats took off down the hall, and Caro couldn't help snort. "He's going to have a rat problem now. That one looks pregnant." Quickly, however, she schooled her expression back into one of interest as Smelzer reappeared holding a digital camera in his hands.

Triumphantly, he ordered, "Take a look at this!" He thrust the camera into Caro's hand.

Looking at him quizzically, she asked, "What do you want me to do with this?"

"Look at the fucking pictures inside! Do I have to spell it out?"

The battery was dead, but a quick word with her cameraman got things hooked up to a power source. She turned it on and looked in the viewfinder for a second. "There's nothing there."

"Yes, there is. Keep lookin', you idiot!" Smelzer cried.

Taking a deep breath and leveling Smelzer with a stare, Caro flipped over the camera and opened the door to the memory card. "Nope. Nothing. Sorry to disappoint you."

"What did you do to it? Did you erase it or something'? I'll sue your ass if you did!" Smelzer carried on and on with spittle flying out of his lips.

Uncle Fred stepped in and calmly took the camera from Caro. "I suggest you mind your manners, Mr. Smelzer. We were all standing here and saw exactly the same thing our cameraman recorded. Nothing has been done to this digital camera." Gaining in volume, he continued, "Now, don't you even dream of trying to blackmail a member of my family ever again! Tanner told me to tell you that the law in Kentucky prohibits the marriage between an uncle and niece, and the penalty for *incest* can be from one year to *life in prison* if prosecuted. He *will* see to it you're prosecuted if you try to come after anyone he cares about again. So, take this travesty of a liquor you've created and shove it up your ass!" He turned away to help the crew disassemble their equipment quickly so they could get out of there, but just as they were heading out the door, he turned to Smelzer once again. The old man had a blank look on his face as Fred asked with a disgusted frown, "What kind of a sick fuck marries his own niece? And you want to accuse *gay people* of being perverted?" He shook his head and marched out the door muttering to himself about bigots and weirdos.

As soon as they were on their way far, far from Payslee Distillery, Caro typed out a message to Eli.

Caro: Mission accomplished ☺ Tell Tanner that Uncle Fred is The Best. Oh, and the "crew" all signed their NDAs. I haven't had this much fun in ages!

Chapter Thirty-Seven

A few days before the inauguration, Tanner, Zoë, Eli, and Caro were all invited to the Lassiters' house for Tanner's birthday. Dr. Lassiter, as it seemed, had a very special gift for his son to celebrate turning thirty... and becoming governor.

Mrs. Lassiter ushered them all into the living room and made sure they were comfortable while her husband went to the other end of the house for something.

When he returned, he presented Tanner with a large basket festooned with an enormous pink bow on top. "Happy birthday, Tanner," he said quietly. "Her name is Maisie."

Up popped a sleepy head of a Black and Tan Coonhound—Tanner's favorite dog of all time. Her ears were so long, they seemed to go on forever, but it was the sweetness of her wise expression that melted Tanner immediately. "Thank you, Daddy. She's fantastic! How old is she? Where'd you get her?"

Chuckling, Dr. Lassiter explained he'd been working with the breeder for years and was thrilled to know she'd be having a litter at just the right time for Tanner. "She's twelve weeks old, and... wow. She is a smart one, son. You're going to have a ball with this little girl."

"Little" was relative, of course. Tanner took in the size of Maisie's enormous paws and knew instantly she'd be at least a sixty- to seventy-pound dog. He carefully plucked her out of the basket and snuggled her up to his face. She gave him a kiss and settled in like he was her new home.

"Maisie, you know what?" Tanner crooned at her. "You're going to be Kentucky's First Dog. So, we'll have to mind our manners."

Right away Zoë scooted over to get in some snuggles, and then everyone started passing her around. Maisie was obviously confident, well-socialized, and quite calm. She seemed perfect.

"We have a bunch of supplies, including a crate for you to take home, so your transition ought to be pretty seamless," Mrs. Lassiter explained. "She really is special. We've had her here for two days, and I'm going to miss her."

***

Maisie, as well as all of her humans, moved into the new house in Frankfort. Chef Oscar and Dante were already ensconced happily in the carriage house on the property, and when Dante met Maisie, he exclaimed, "Well, y'all don't have a baby for me to care for quite yet, so I'll have to practice on this beautiful little girl." He took to his duties with a vengeance, giving everyone a great sense that he'd make the best manny ever when the time came. He also filled in around the house in whatever capacity he was needed. Eli's first hires were working out splendidly.

***

Now that the election was over, Eli expected his sister to head back to New York. "When do you plan to go, Caro?" he asked on the eve of the inauguration.

Caro looked at him with a serious expression and asked, "Does it bother you that I'm here?"

"Heavens, no! I love having you around," he answered honestly.

"Enough to find me a permanent position with Tanner's staff? Or maybe something for Zoë?" She looked slightly embarrassed. "The fact is, Eli, I always thought New York was the be-all, end-all, but I've enjoyed every minute I've spent here in Kentucky. I don't want to leave, and I love all of my new friends. They seem... real."

And so, it was decided, much to Zoë's delight, that Caro would stay on as a personal assistant to the First Lady. It was a catch-all job that wasn't all that different from what she'd been doing all along, and it made both of them as happy as can be. Caro also bought herself a house nearby and had as much fun furnishing it as she had with the governor's new place. With this one, she was able to take her time a bit more, however.

***

Tanner's inaugural address was so moving and eloquent; news stations around the country broadcast it far beyond Kentucky. Naturally, this practice had been given a healthy boost by Eli who was already planning in the back of his mind for Tanner's next political move—running for president. Once again, Tanner would have to wait until he reached the minimum age requirement of thirty-five, so it would make sense to have him run for a second term as governor in the meantime. He would be a year into his second term before reaching thirty-five.

Photo after photo of the handsome new governor and his stunning wife appeared on television and all over the internet. People just couldn't get enough of them. In several of the photos another couple was identified as Eli and Caro Whittaker, Tanner's Chief of Staff and Zoë's Personal Assistant. This led many folks to assume they were another married couple. No one paid a lot of attention to them, other than to remark on their attractiveness.

***

After all of the speeches and the celebrating at the inaugural ball finally wound to a close, Tanner, Zoë, and Eli finally headed for home. Pumped up and exhausted simultaneously, they were more than ready for some quiet and some time to do their own celebrating.

"I have a plan, gentlemen," Zoë announced as they climbed the stairs to their magnificent master suite. She gave them both a sultry look.

Entering the suite, Tanner sighed happily as Eli closed in on the two of them, wrapping them in his arms. "What's your idea, Zoë? Something new?"

Zoë's eyes sparkled with mischief and desire. "You two are the most handsome, most wonderful men in the world. I am so lucky." She kissed Tanner and then Eli. "I want you both at the same time."

Frowning slightly, Eli asked, "We've done that plenty of times, Zoë. You know we love it, so what's different?" He gently kissed her neck as his hand reached into Tanner's jacket to feel his warm body.

"You misunderstand, Eli. I want you both inside me together. Especially if we're going to be making babies, I want you in my pussy *with* Tanner. We'll all make love to each other at the very same time."

Tanner pulled back and gave her a heated look. "I love the idea!" He looked at Eli. "You good with it?"

Eli looked so excited he might be about to swallow his own tongue. He croaked, "Oh, God, Zoë. If you think you can do it, I can't think of anything better."

Giggling, she ordered, "Then get yourselves out of those tuxes and let's figure this out, alright?" She turned around and presented the back of her ball gown, "Someone unzip me, please!"

Tearing at his bowtie as he simultaneously kicked off his shoes, Tanner asked, "Have you read about this one, or are we going in blind here?"

"I've done my research. Books, videos, you name it. I'm a little nervous though."

Eli kissed her bare shoulder and whispered, "We're all in this together. We'll figure it out. It's a wonderful idea."

Divested of their finery that was now all in a heap on the bedroom floor, the three of them began kissing and stroking each other. Eli dropped to his knees and began alternately licking his lovers. He would take Tanner into his mouth as he fingered Zoë, and then he'd pull away and probe at Zoë's clit while stroking Tanner. Zoë, meanwhile, kissed the daylights out of Tanner as she reached around and fondled his firm butt. Tanner ran his hands through Eli's hair and moaned with pleasure.

Zoë gave Tanner a gentle shove toward the bed. "Lie back," she ordered. When he got comfortable, she straddled him with her ass in the air and began to suck his steely erection. She reached a hand out to Eli to bring him in closer and stroked him with one hand as she continued to fellate Tanner.

Eli stood beside the bed and finger fucked Zoë as she played with her men. Their soft moans and groans filled the air. Finally, she asked Eli, "Could you get us some lube, please?"

As Eli fished around in the cabinet for a bottle, Zoë positioned herself over Tanner's mouth. "Make me as wet as you can," she demanded. Tanner was more than willing to accommodate that request and smashed his mouth over her, licking and probing her as he used his fingers to spread her moisture around. "Yes. Yes!" she moaned and shattered as an orgasm burst through her. Finally, she caught her breath and then turned around over Tanner in a reverse cowgirl position. Slowly, she sunk down on him and engulfed him inside her.

Tanner grabbed her by the hips and thrust up into her over and over again. He knew he had to maintain, but it just felt too good.

"Okay, slow down Tanner. Now we're going to get to the best part," she breathed on a moan. "Are you ready, Eli?"

Eli stood patiently next to the bed relishing the sight of Tanner and Zoë as they made love. His erection was like titanium, and he couldn't wait to join in. He was about to use the bottle of lube when a different idea crossed his mind. So, he scooted as close to the couple as he could and bent down, putting his face right where Tanner and Zoë were joined. First, he played with Zoë's clit with his tongue, causing her to gasp in delight. Then he began licking every part of Tanner's dick he could reach. Back and forth he went between his lovers as they fucked and he licked them. When they were sufficiently drenched with his saliva and Zoë's arousal, he stood and started probing her pussy with his finger. First one slid in alongside Tanner's dick, causing all three of them to groan. Then another finger, though it met with a lot of resistance.

"Relax, Zoë," Eli whispered. "You can do this. You feel so good around my finger with Tan inside you." He felt her relax and shoved in his second finger.

Zoë hissed and Eli stopped. "Are you alright?" he asked with concern.

"Yes, fine. Keep going, Eli! I want you in me too. Use your dick!"

So, Eli gave Tanner's erection a long stroke with his fingers as he pulled them out of Zoë, caressing Tanner's balls as he pulled away. "Here goes," he warned.

Eli grasped his own erection and rubbed it up against Tanner's, slowly feeding it into Zoë's opening the way he'd done with his fingers. His broad tip was a lot larger, though, and it was going to take some doing to broach the tight barrier. "Relax. We love you, Zoë," he whispered as he kissed her. He kept a close look on her face as he slowly pushed inside.

Zoë hissed, causing Eli to stop. "No, keep going," she ordered. "It hurts, but for some reason I love it!" She hissed again and grabbed Eli around his shoulders. Tanner still had a firm grip on her hips, but he'd stopped thrusting until Eli could get situated inside too.

"Almost there," Eli reassured her. "Just a little more now. God, it feels so amazing! I'm literally fucking both of you at the same time." With what felt like a colossal effort, he slowly kept up his pushing into Zoë.

"Aaugh," cried Zoë at last. "Ohmygod!" She was breathing hard and had her eyes squinched shut against the pain. "Is that it? Are you all the way in, Eli?" The truth was, it hurt like hell, but it was also the single most exciting thing she could imagine. With superhuman effort, she relaxed her muscles and took a deep breath. "Okay. I'll be alright now."

And then began the most exquisitely wonderful pain ever. Both men alternated thrusting in and out. The feeling was extraordinary. She knew they could feel their dicks against each other, and she was the one holding them in place. Gradually, the stinging and burning went away, leaving Zoë with intense pleasure instead. "Ohmygod, I love this!" she exclaimed, causing the worry to disappear from Eli's expression. Tanner reached around from behind Zoë and started playing with her clit as the two men continued their thrusting.

"This is the best way for a three-way," Tanner exclaimed. "Let's make a baby out of this." He sped up his fingers on Zoë's nub and relished the feel of Eli rubbing against him while they were squeezed by Zoë. "I'm close! Is anyone else getting close?"

Zoë immediately shuddered with an orgasm.

"Yes," groaned Eli in a strangled cry. "Let it go, Tan." With one massive push, Eli shook with his release at the same time Tanner gave up his own.

Once they relaxed into an exhausted jumble, Zoë announced, "That was way better than anything I ever read about. It was amazing."

After the three of them took a long, hot shower together, they fell back into bed. Zoë kissed her men and was asleep within minutes. Tanner and Eli also kissed each other good night and fell into an exceptionally satisfied slumber.

***

Nine months later, almost to the minute, Zoë gave birth to a little girl who looked like a junior version of her. They named her Stella Whittaker Lassiter. She grew up in a house filled with love. Maisie adored her.

A year after Stella's birth, Zoë had a baby boy. And so on, until the enormous house was bursting with children—four of them.

Chapter Thirty-Eight

As Tanner celebrated his thirty-fifth birthday and was into his second term, a change seemed to overtake him. He'd made an extremely popular governor. Zoë was one of the most beloved first ladies the state had ever had, and he was proud of how she juggled the causes she championed while being a fantastic mother to their children. But somehow, now that he had this incredibly beautiful and growing family, the burning desire to become president didn't seem at all appealing any longer. The idea of crisscrossing the country to campaign had lost its luster and now sounded like a terrible chore. He wanted to be home with his wife, his husband, and their gorgeous babies. He decided it was time to discuss his feelings with Eli and Zoë.

Over beers—and a sweet tea for Zoë, who seemed to be perpetually pregnant—Tanner laid all his cards on the table. "I don't want to run anymore. I'm done. Being mayor of Honeybee Hollow was wonderful, being governor of Kentucky has been a dream come true, but that's it for me. No more campaigning. I'm done."

"Oh, thank God," sighed Zoë at the exact same time that Eli laughed, "It's about time you figured it out, Tan."

"You're not surprised or upset?" Tanner asked looking at them alternately.

Zoë smiled like a Madonna as Eli explained, "It's been clear for some time now that your heart's not in the rat race anymore. Leave it to the career politicians and the power-seekers to go down that road. You can serve the country in many ways without sacrificing any more of your privacy and time you'd prefer to spend with your loved ones." He paused and looked fondly at Zoë, who absently rubbed her belly. "Zoë and I have talked about it, and we decided to give you time to figure it out for yourself. We'll continue to support anything you want to do—even if it's nothing at all. Back when we were at Princeton, being the future president sounded like the coolest thing ever, but the times have changed, and that's not a job I'd exactly want for you any longer."

"You're not sad you'll have to stop being a kingmaker?" teased Tanner.

"Not in the least. I've enjoyed being your Chief of Staff way more, actually. And we can always figure out what we can do to fulfill our lives." Looking smug, Eli continued, "It helps being a billionaire—sort of takes the pressure off, you know?"

***

So, during the final years that Tanner served as governor, the three of them plotted and planned their futures.

Zoë wanted to champion her literacy cause. The teacher in her wouldn't let that one slide. So, they established a foundation she and Caro ran together.

Eli simply wanted to be a house-husband and wallow in the chaos of their children. He'd never felt so fulfilled as when he got up to change a diaper at two in the morning and rocked a baby back to sleep. He wouldn't dream of turning down Dante's help, however, as the man seemed to have answers for every crazy question that came up. As the children grew older, he taught them all how to fish, and they loved it.

And Tanner became an expert political contributor who was sought out by the major TV networks to give his opinions on world and national events. His speech-making abilities along

with his incredibly good looks caused everyone to pay attention to him. He also began writing political commentary books
that quickly rose to the top of the best sellers' lists. He had an
unending supply of opinions to share.

All of them were staunch supporters of the LGBTQ community, but they never did make their three-way marriage public
beyond their families and closest friends. It was just no one
else's business, and they didn't want their kids to be bullied or
teased about it.

So, they continued to live in Frankfort in the house that
Eli had bought them. It was a great house—with lots of room
for children to play with their sweet hound dog. And the walls
seemed to burst with love.

The End

Ready for more MMF stories?
Check out *Just Curious*:
And don't miss *Compelling Urges*:

Acknowledgments

I would have liked to have thanked the Kentucky Distillers' Association for all of their great information. Unfortunately, after I did as much online research about them as I could, I contacted them with specific questions. They blew me off. So, if I've misrepresented anything in this book, I'm sorry. I did the best I could and made up the rest. There seems to be something slightly poisonous about saying, "I'm an author and have a few questions..." People clam up and run the other direction.

I thought a few times while writing this book that I was nuts to take on the story about a politician. It was with every shred of effort I could muster to make certain that Tanner didn't represent one party or one set of ideals. I hope that didn't come across as shallow, but I knew as soon as my own agendas crept in, half of my readers would be pissed off. My political beliefs are my own, and I don't care to share them. In much the same way as the main characters decided to keep their relationship status to themselves, I believe we all have a right to privacy—even if you're voluntarily in the public eye.

I toyed for a long time with the idea of making this a two-book series, the second one of which being Tanner's road to the White House. However, as world events went from bad to worse as I wrote, I decided I couldn't do it to him. He's such a lovable man, I wanted to keep him in a protective bubble with his family instead. They are all too nice for that kind of life.

I need to thank everyone who helped me get this book out to you. My editor Dayna, my longtime proofreader Mattie who is lots of fun to work with, my fearless beta reader Susan who has lovely ideas and boosts my ego, and my talented graphics advisor Shannon who gave tremendous advice. You make a great team!

And, naturally, my husband. He listens to more goofiness that spills out of my brain and helps me stick it all together into a cohesive idea. Well done.

Thank you, dear readers, for reading my books!

Please stay tuned with information on deals and releases by signing up for my newsletter. https://landing.mailerlite.com/webforms/landing/m6f3i7

And please, leave a review when you finish a book. All authors will thank you.

Books by Ariella Talix

Porter the Importer: The Drummonds- Prequel

The story of the Drummond family begins with Molly Drummond and Porter Delaney in this prequel novella. Find out how Porter became the Importer and how Molly started her naughty boutique. Fall in love with Porter and the Drummonds.

Make Believe: The Drummonds- Book One

Lily Drummond's emotional love story with Finn Reilly is romantic suspense with plenty of humor and cute dogs. A page-turner! It's a Canterbury Tales-like saga with a host of interesting characters.

The Artist: The Drummonds- Book Two

This is David Drummond's story with Amelia Hernandez. It takes place mostly in Paris, and it will pull at your heartstrings. Imagination and beauty from page to page. A sizzling, sexy love story and much, much more.

Save Her: Lovers in Louisville- Book One

This series is a spin-off from The Drummonds. Your favorite characters appear again in supporting roles. *Save Her* is full of suspense and a couple you will adore. Åse Halvorsen is a beautiful jewelry designer, and Gunnar Dahl is a famous mystery writer with a secret.

Saving Him: Lovers in Louisville- Book Two

Sibylla Eliana Xenopoulos (Sibley) was Åse's roommate and best friend in college. She returns to Louisville for a great opportunity and finds love with Gunnar's buddy Leo Spanos. Their chemistry is off the charts, but danger lurks in the shadows.

Savor This: Lovers in Louisville- Book Three

In this passionate and unpredictable story, Halden Dahl, Gunnar's younger brother, is a successful glass artist and total ladies' man. Handsome and talented with an ego as big as all outdoors, has he finally met his match? The answer is yes when he sets his sights on Madison Lassiter—beautiful, passionate, and extremely focused.

The Rule of 3

Since no one actually lives in Louisville in this book, it became a standalone spin-off from the popular "Lovers in Louisville" series. It's a departure from my earlier works in that this one is an MMF story. Tanner Lassiter, Zoë Deliban, and a new character, Eli Whittaker, all make for a delightful book about ambition, loyalty, and the deepest, most enduring kind of love.

Just Curious

This standalone MMF story is about Willa, a gorgeous and highly successful writer who falls for her billionaire neighbor Jackson and his life-long friend Casey. An old acquaintance causes them trouble, and the seriousness of it escalates to a dangerous level. The setting is mostly in southern California, but they do some globe-trotting as well.

Compelling Urges

A loose spin-off from *Just Curious*, this MMF story is also set in San Diego County. Bodhi Monaghan, Cooper Houston and Ivy Chambers navigate some troubled waters before they can manage their life together as a triad. Doubts and trust issues plague them as well as a strange and interesting character who is bent on claiming or possibly ruining Bodhi.

The Golden Rush

This is an MMF romance set during the 1849 California Gold Rush. Six men travel across the country, creating an unbreakable bond of friendship and find themselves in the right place at the right time. Jasper Langley and Royal Dawson eventually meet Adeline Hart, and both fall head over heels for her. It is a moving tale of perseverance, compassion, and sheer grit.

Fiddle and Fire

Sequel to The Golden Rush- Coming in 2022

Each book is a standalone with a guaranteed HEA, but it's more fun if you read them in order. All books are intended for mature readers only.

https://www.ariellatalix.com/